MY NAME IS MARK!

Daniel M. Perry

ISBN-10: 1519636202
ISBN-13: 978-1519636201

DEDICATION

This story is dedicated to my mother Anna Mae Perry Pallazzo. She has been the definition of Faith for me providing the foundation for my own beliefs, commitment and understanding of Jesus, and the wonderful Grace of reconciliation.

CONTENTS

PRELUDE

*And a certain woman whose brother had died was there.
And, coming, she prostrated herself before Jesus*

and says to him, 'Son of David, have mercy on me.'

But the disciples rebuked her. And Jesus, being angered,

went off with her into the garden where the tomb was,

and straightway a great cry was heard from the tomb.

And going near, Jesus rolled away the stone from

the door of the tomb. And straightway, going where

the youth was, he stretched forth his hand and raised him,

seizing his hand. But the youth, looking upon Him, loved

Him and began to beseech him that he might be with Him.

- The Secret Gospel of Mark Chapter 10:35

And he that betrayeth him had given them a token saying,

Whomever I shall kiss, that same is he; take him and lead

him away safely. And as soon as he was come he goeth

straightway to him and saith, "Master, Master;" and kissed

him. And they laid their hands on him and took him. And

one of them that stood by drew a sword, and smote a

servant of the High Priest, and cut off his ear. And Jesus

answered and said unto them, Are ye come out, as against

a thief, with swords and with staves to take me? I was daily

with you in the Temple teaching, and ye took me not;

but the scriptures must be fulfilled. And they all forsook

him and fled. And there followed him a certain young man,

having a linen cloth cast about his naked body;

and the men laid hold on him. And he left the linen cloth,

and fled from them naked.

- The Gospel of Mark Chapter 14:44-52

Passover Night

Two guards lunged at me. I stumbled backward from the bush I was hiding behind. I tried to run away, my legs twisting and turning awkwardly without the coordination I was so used to knowing just last week. I felt the sharpness of the roots on the soles of my feet, yet felt no pain as I ran, tried to run, tried to escape their grasp. Grabbing my arms, they seized me by the burial linen that was to be my garment for eternity. It was made from fine cloth, exquisitely woven for the burial of a beloved family member. The garment was now partly on the ground under foot and partly twisted around the legs of the guards grabbing me. I turned and contorted in my struggle to free my body from their grasp. The very linen that was to comfort me through my timeless journey now wrapped its weave around the legs of the guards. The threads loosened their grip on me, growing tighter around the legs of the guards; as if moving on its own volition, letting me free, enabling my escape from its clutches and the arms of the guards. I ran only one step before stumbling to my knees. I lurched forward and sprang upward, my legs trying to move as fast as they could. Looking back; I see the fine linen wrapped around the legs of the two Roman guards. They're rolling on the ground trying to break free from the wrap that has fallen them like an ax to a tree. I was free. I was naked, but at least I was free. And I was alive. Again.

I died two days ago. It feels like I've just been asleep except my body hurts. My sister Sarah said I was found off the road to Bethpage, in a ravine, with my neck broken. She would be with me here at my tomb had I not tricked her into going home to get clothes and help. Sarah said everyone thought it was such a tragic accident. Mother's beside herself with grief, and Father wasn't acting right, giving in to fits of anger, and rants of rage against any little thing that crossed his path. He's unbearable to be around, but all would be better now that I'm back. All would be fine. Mother would return to health, Father would forgive God. Life could return to normal now that I've come back from the dead. Any of the trouble with this man Jesus would work itself out once the people saw that he had raised me from the dead. Sarah begged me to return home with her, but I couldn't. I had to see Jesus before returning home. I had to speak with him before returning to my old life. I didn't want him to leave me earlier when he woke me in my tomb. I wanted to become one of his disciples then and there. Who else would I follow? He raised me from death. He is The Christ. The boy I was last week, Jonas, no longer exists. I had been made new. I've been reborn, and this scared me. I didn't want anyone but my family to find I've regained the breath of life. No, if people found out, my name would be remembered with that of Lazarus from Bethany. I had no desire to be famous like that. I'd heard of Lazarus. My village of Bethpage wasn't far from Bethany. I tried to imagine waking from death like that, and now it's happened. My friends and I wondered what his life was like. Would he ever die again? Would I? How old would he become, having cheated death? I didn't want people to look at me like I was an oddity; risen from death. I wanted to stay dead to this world and follow Jesus - learn his teachings. I want to let everyone know He is sent from God. His words are like bread to the hungry and music to the ears.

Now, from my perch half-hidden by this small bush overlooking the Garden of Gethsemane, I can see a gathering of four men, Jesus and three of his followers. Yes, there's Simon Peter. I recognize him from our walk to Jerusalem last week.

And the other two, John and James I think. I remember talking with them as well. But now, Jesus had just yelled at his disciples for falling asleep.

It was someone named Malchus who killed me. That is, I think he killed me. Somehow I saw him; but I also saw my own body lying in the middle of the road; like I was floating in the air looking down. I don't know if that was a memory or a dream. I've been dead not asleep, so the image I remember is confusing. I remember getting hit hard in the back of my head, and hearing the crack of my neck breaking; a dull thud echoing through my skull. Had I fallen from the road? Was I kicked by the mule? The snap of my neck was the last sound I heard. I felt it more than heard it; "*Crack!*" echoing once or twice around my brain. I was afraid and trying to hurry home. I had a feeling of dread, a knot in my stomach twisting inside me. I knew I'd heard something bad. I thought about nothing but reaching the safety of home. I was going to tell Mother about what I'd overheard, and wait for Father to return home and form some kind of plan to help Jesus. He would know what to do. That's all I thought about every step of the way back. It was dusk and the setting sun slowly dimmed the remaining light of day. I was pulling on the reins imploring the donkey to move faster as we climbed a hill halfway home. I hadn't heard the rustling of footsteps, and it wouldn't have done much good if I did. Malchus ambushed me as I crested the hill, jumping out from behind a large rock and smashing my head with a boulder just as big.

That was a few days ago. And now, something seems wrong here. Jesus just yelled at his disciples for being asleep. Jesus had been kneeling off by himself a stones throw away when I first climbed up the hill. I didn't seen him until he walked to them and raised his voice to wake them up. I settled

7

into a hiding place behind some bushes to watch and wait for the right time. The full moon illuminated the Garden with a dull light that seemed to make the small clearing glow. I had to try to find a way to talk with Jesus. I couldn't go home, not now, not after I'd been raised from the dead. He had to let me follow him. I may be young but I know I can help somehow. I can testify to the truth that Jesus is The Christ.

I thought about just running up to him, beg him to take me into his group, let me follow; teach me all I need to know about life. I heard Jesus say *"Rise up, let us go; lo, he that betrayeth me is at hand."* I looked around and didn't see anyone right away, but then the glow of lamps and torches getting closer appeared from the path out of the Garden. Shortly, a group of Roman guards approached, led by the disciple of Jesus named Judas. And there's Malchus as well. They're with a mob carrying torches, lanterns and staves. I recognize some priests and elders from The Temple. Caiaphas must have sent twenty priests with Malchus to arrest Jesus.

There they were, the two conspirators, bringing the authorities to arrest Jesus. I overheard their plot; and I knew personally the lengths Malchus would take to please his master. He had hate in his heart. His only master was Caiaphas, and Caiaphas wanted Jesus arrested. Jesus raised a commotion at the Temple the Saturday before I died. I saw it. Father had his table and bird coops overturned and all the businessmen were scolded for making the house of God into a marketplace. Then I saw Judas return to the Temple later while I was packing the mule to return home. I sinned by eavesdropping as I listened in on his conversation with Malchus, hidden behind a column in the Temple courtyard. It went something like this: "Good evening, I believe you're a servant of the High Priests, are you not?"

"I'm the head servant for Caiaphas." Malchus replied, just a few feet away from where I was hiding. Judas seemed unhappy.

"I have information I believe Caiaphas would be interested in."

"Yes, and what might this be about that I may tell my master? Is it something worth taking the time of the High Priest?"

"I'm Judas of Iscariot. I know the Sanhedrin have a desire to arrest Jesus of Nazareth, and I believe I could be of some assistance"

"You have heard correctly. There's been some discussion. Jesus has made a name for himself teaching at the Temple in the mornings. But Caiaphas would be interested to know where he spends his nights."

"That could be a different place each night." Judas replied. "Sometimes we make camp, weather permitting. Other nights we may be offered the comfort of a house or courtyard by someone we've met at Temple. I've been surprised by the kindness and generosity of people. Perhaps Caiaphas will feel generous if he knew I could obtain this information each day this week."

"Between us, generosity is not one of my master's abundant qualities, but he would be pleased if he had this knowledge. Forgive my boldness, but I don't understand your motivation; why turn your master in to Caiaphas?"

"Many reasons have been simmering like a cauldron on a slow fire. The contents are boiling now, and the time has come for change. Jesus talks of taking care of the widows and orphans, yet allows an expensive oil be wasted on him. Why? It could have been sold to help our mission. He speaks of the Kingdom of Heaven here on earth, but does nothing against the oppression of Jews by the Romans. Who will deliver the Jews from this oppression if not he? He just upsets the Pharisees by questioning their behavior. Believe me, I don't want any harm to come to him, but I believe a confrontation with the Sanhedrin might influence him. Perhaps he can work with the Council, rather than against them. I'm only asking you to arrange an introduction for me. If Jesus is indeed the Messiah, then it's time to lead our people against the Romans. Perhaps something will happen if he is forced to deal with the Sanhedrin."

Malchus asked Judas to wait outside the chamber of councils while he went to speak with Caiaphas. A few moments passed and Judas was shown into the chamber room. Soon, the door opened and Malchus began to escort Judas back down the corridor. They started toward the courtyard entry to leave the Temple. I overheard some details of their conversation.

Judas spoke, "I'll return after the Passover Feast, at the end of this week and lead you to him at night, away from the daytime crowds. I don't know how the other disciples will react. If you can arrange for a small number of elders and High Priests to be available as we lead the Romans to him, perhaps we'll avoid any unnecessary problems, and this business can be finished without problems from the people."

Malchus added "Remember to keep an ear open for blasphemy. After all, he's just a man, but he speaks as if he is something more. Jesus is a dangerous person to the Jewish nation. Perhaps it'd be better for all Jews if he were punished for comparing himself to God. Any evidence leading to charges of blasphemy would be richly rewarded. Any evidence of law-breaking would be pleasing to Caiaphas and the Sanhedrin."

I couldn't believe what I'd heard. Judas gave no reply at

first as if thinking about something. Then he said his current agreement with Caiaphas would be to hand Jesus over to the Sanhedrin, and that was all he was willing to do. They started walking down the hallway, and I made my way back to the entryway from the interior of the courtyard, on the other side of the columns.

And now, behind this bush, I'm witnessing the reality of the plot I overheard. Where were the other disciples? Why were they not here? Did they flee when they saw this mob approaching? There're only three men here to fight. What help could I give? I could be of no help, a boy, not a man, wrapped in burial linens. The other disciples should be close by, where were they?

Judas has moved in front of the mob leading them directly toward Jesus. *"...he that betrayeth me is at hand."* How did Jesus know?

Jesus took a step forward asking *"Whom seek ye?"*

Malchus spoke up, sneering "We seek Jesus of Nazareth."

Jesus replied *"I am he."* When he said this; the ground shook. Immediately, as if on cue, the whole mob of men fell backward onto the ground. I don't know why, but they all lost their footing as if standing on a carpet and had that carpet pulled out from under them. Jesus, still standing, asked again *"Whom seek ye?"*

Again, Malchus was the first to reply "Jesus of Nazareth!" with anger and irritation in his voice, picking himself off the ground.

Jesus said *"I have told you I am he; if therefore ye seek me; let these men go their way."*

Judas stepped directly in front of Jesus, saying "Master, master." and he kissed him on the cheek. The kiss was the signal for the Roman guards. They moved forward to grab the arms of Jesus. Malchus slithered his way around behind Jesus to get out of the way. I imagine he felt rather smug, leading the elders and authorities here. He would surely be rewarded by Caiaphas for his loyalty and hard work. This would be a real feather in his cap. Malchus stood there, looking down his nose at this holy man who had done nothing but heal the sick and teach to our Jewish law.

Malchus didn't expect what happened next. The disciple standing closest to Jesus flew to action as the guards grabbed Jesus. I think it was Simon Peter. He drew his sword, and struck Malchus hard on the right side of his head cutting off his ear. His scream rang out; he dropped to his knees and clutched the side of his head. This stopped the Roman guards in their tracks. They drew their swords to retaliate, starting toward the disciple.

Then Jesus held his hands up, one to the guards, the other to his disciple saying *"Are ye come out, as against a thief? With swords and with staves to take me?"*

He faced his disciple and said *"Put up thy sword into the sheath; the cup which my Father hath given me, shall I not drink?"*

He stooped down to the crouched body of Malchus, now crying stifled sobs and moans of pain from the sudden removal of his ear. Jesus reached down and placed his hand over the dangling stub of cartilage while continuing to speak. *"I was daily with you in the Temple teaching, and ye took me not; but the scriptures must be fulfilled."* He stood and looked toward the direction of his three followers. They had started backing away slowly when the guards stopped in their tracks. They continued to slowly gain distance as Jesus knelt down to touch the injury of the one who led the mob here to arrest him. They were practically running away now as Jesus allowed the Roman guards to escort him down the path.

From my hiding spot here I see Malchus, fallen and kneeling on the ground clutching his right ear, blood staining his fingers and hands. He's kneeling there wild-eyed. His sobbing has stopped and he is frantically feeling the side of his head. He's just staring at Jesus being led away by the guards, eyes wide, mouth open. I don't understand this confused look on his face. Then I see the side of his head and his ear, fully intact, not dangling by the sliver of skin like it was seconds ago. His ear is fully healed now, the bleeding has stopped. He kneels there no longer wild-eyed from the shock of having his ear cut off, but from the shock of having it healed. He was healed instantly when Jesus touched his ear, the man he worked so hard to get arrested had healed him.

Or maybe he's looking a little wild-eyed because he's happened to see me crouching beside this bush watching the whole scene. What? How? The very boy he chased; the very boy he caught; the very boy he killed. He snapped my neck like a chicken and threw me down that hill. How could this be? He had walked up to my unconscious body lying on the roadside after hitting me with a rock, grabbed my head and twisted my neck until he heard that final snap. He made everything look like an accident, and made sure I told no one about the plan to arrest Jesus. He's seen me now and he is again wild-eyed with his own fear. He points up with his right hand, his eyes filled with confusion and disbelief, knowing I died a few days ago, knowing he killed me, knowing I knew the truth and must be stopped, miracle or no miracle. He pointed up at me for the two Roman guards to grab.

Thursday Morning, Last Week.

"Jonas. Finish eating breakfast, take this bundle and load it on the mule with the dove cages. Go on, I have an important meeting this morning." Abram spoke as I rose from the floor and took the bundle which was obviously some kind of fabric wrapped up in a linen cover. I grabbed a piece of sweet bread and headed for the stable attached to the courtyard of our house. "This will be a good week, mark my words." Abram went on talking to himself more than to my mother or sister. "We should do very well this Pessach. There's many more pilgrims this year." he spoke softly wrapping himself a small loaf of bread, a couple of figs, and some olives in a cloth of linen for the trip into Jerusalem. "May God bless our family. May God bless our business. Finally, we'll be able to move to the city, Elizabeth. The Jewish people are flourishing there. People come to the Temple in waves. You know, business would be better if we lived in the city. I'm doing this for us. It'll work out for the best. I've got to go. I don't want to be late. There're important matters to discuss with the High Priest; very important, you'll see, this will be for the best." His voice trailed off softly speaking to himself, "Many more pilgrims this year." Then he called out "Sarah, do we have enough bread for our guests this morning? Bake extra bread today; we have two families camping in the field, and there may be more seeking shelter."

I walked into the stable. "Hey there, fella." I said as I patted the mule on his backside, rubbing his back from the neck down, petting his mane, wafting some feed in front of his nose to entice him out of the stall. We had a second mule and its foal, a small colt that had never been ridden. The mules were used to till the garden and turn the press that crushed our olives when we made oil. The colt was too young for riding and my sister treated it more like her pet than a beast of labor. I threw the blanket over the mules' back and tied down the four dove cages, two on either side strapped together hanging over the back of the mule. Placing the bundle Father gave me on top of the blanket; I strapped it down with his floor mat and table cloth for the merchant stall. I looked up to see my Father walking toward me holding his book of receipts and tying his coin purse to his tunic belt. I put another dove into the cage when he walked around the side of the mule. "Jonas, tie the mule and colt out front while you clean out the stall. Be sure to help your mother and sister with the bread this morning before school, we'll want to bake more today." With that Abram swatted the mule and started his early morning trek to the Temple. Before getting too far away, he called back "Don't let me hear the rabbi tell of you whispering to the other students when you should be studying. You have less time than you think before your bar mitzvah." Abram flicked the mule again and continued down the road to Jerusalem.

Walking along the road leading from Bethpage to Jerusalem, Abram thought about what he'd say. First impressions were important and he needed to leave Caiaphas with a lasting first impression. 'Good morning, your honor. No, no. I should say Peace and Blessings onto the House of David, or simply God be with you, Rabbi. Yes, that's what I'll say; God be with you Rabbi; simple, yet respectful.' Abram tried to imagine the meeting he'd managed to arrange. He thought through his offer, thought about any possible objections he might receive, though he really doubted a man like Caiaphas would refuse the possibility of profit. Abram even discussed it with Malchus, who became keen to make the introduction, to arrange the meeting and receive the gratitude of his master, as well as gifts of olive oil from Abram. Abram had seen the easiest way to gain an audience with the High Priest was through the servant that knew him so well, namely, Malchus. Abram had his idea last year during the Feast of Weeks, and had been thinking of it since. At that time he'd given Malchus a small jar of olive oil, and a jar of spice to give to the Temple priests. He did this formally as a way to "thank" the High Council for allowing merchants into the Temple. He mainly did it to buy favor with the High Priests and make himself known. The Sanhedrin had approved the practice of allowing merchants to set up their tables in the corridor and courtyard of the Temple. They did this to accommodate the growing number of pilgrims visiting Jerusalem three times a year, but more importantly did it to insure the collection of the Temple tax. The day after Abram presented his gift, Malchus offered him a table closer to the men's entry to the Courtyard of Gentiles. His table had been located near the women's Temple entry, and many local women brought their own doves from home for sacrifice. Malchus said Abrams gift was appreciated and moving his merchant table was a simple act of gratitude for the olive oil and spice. Something in the way Malchus spoke made Abram think the High Priests never received the spice. He would seek to gain favor with the High Council through this head servant.

Upon moving closer to the men's entry; Abram found he was busier and made more profit the rest of that week; simply because traffic by male pilgrims increased. He was pleased and the dreams of making more money, moving his family to Jerusalem, gaining a better life for his children were planted. His table was now one of the first available to purchase doves for sacrifices. The Temple tax was collected at tables located directly at the entry into the courtyard. There were a few merchants and priests collecting the half shekel tax, but they often needed to refer a pilgrim to a money changer to convert a foreign currency into the shekel. Abram had become familiar with many different currencies and thought he would do well adding that aspect of business to his dove sales. He also wondered how much it would cost him in "gifts" to begin collecting the Temple tax for the Sanhedrin. This could be profitable since a fee was the merchants providing this service. He noticed Caiaphas took pride in his appearance, wearing robes of the finest dyed wool, and the air lingered with a smell of exotic perfume as he passed through the corridors of the Temple. Abram was able to trade for these items. He enjoyed trading for silk and other fineries. Every now and then he'd be able to trade for shells from the sea. These could be crushed to make a royal blue dye that brought a very good price when sold. He offered Malchus some spices to arrange a meeting with Caiaphas, and today he was bringing Caiaphas a small bale of silk to thank him for his time. He was hoping these 'gifts' might secure him a favorable table spot during Passover week and future festival weeks. He would put in motion his plan to become a Temple tax collector. It seemed the usual way of doing business at the Temple was to buy off a few priests. There were so many priests though, and developing a relationship with one of the Sanhedrin could prove difficult. So Abram felt doubly blessed by this arranged meeting with none other than Caiaphas. He would become a money changer for pilgrims, sell doves for sacrifices, and collect the Temple tax. Abram could only hope his gifts would satisfy Caiaphas, and satisfy the price of obtaining this prime "real estate". If all worked out, he could finally move his family to Jerusalem. The mule plodded along loaded with the silk and doves.

Traveling a short distance, Abram passed the marketplace of Bethpage. His thoughts reminisced to his first stall there. When his Father died, the family farm was divided between Abram and his three brothers. Not being very fond of working the farm, Abram chose a plot of land where the road from Bethany met the road from Bethpage to Jerusalem. A small mud brick house was already built there, but Abram expanded on it, built a wall to create a courtyard and eventually added a stable. It came with a grove of olive trees and grapes on the rolling hillside in front of the house. On the other side of that hill lay the Cedron valley. The family's burial tombs were on the other side of the olive grove, set back in the hills that descend into the valley. On the other side of the Cedron valley was the garden of Gethsemane, halfway up the lower slope of the Mount of Olives.

As Abram had helped his brothers with their barley fields during harvest, he was helped by nephews and nieces during olive and grape harvest. The family shared in the delights of the earth. His brothers kept a few sheep for Abram with their flock, and together they celebrated the feasts of their Jewish religion. His brothers supported his decision to become a merchant. They helped provide most of the doves Abram sold outside the synagogue when he started his business. It wasn't until after his first olive harvest and pressing that Abram was able to begin selling olives, olive oil and doves without borrowing from his brothers. He repaid them with two bales of silk obtained in a trade. He'd been grateful for his family's help, and knew they would always be there for him. He thought how proud his Father would be.

At these thoughts, he said a short prayer of thanks for his loved ones and the grace of his success. He was sure he was blessed. Abram had been able to make a good living as a merchant. He gained a good reputation being honest, fair and willing to barter if you couldn't afford to buy. He thought himself a good Jew, followed the laws of his faith; taught his son the value of being obedient to God. He enjoyed bartering with the different pilgrims that would pass through Bethpage on their way to Jerusalem. He enjoyed meeting people and knew there could be something of value gained from striking up a conversation. Whether that conversation was with a Persian traveler or a Gentile passing by, it made no difference to Abram. In this way he was different from many other Jews as they often shunned foreigners, especially Gentiles. He'd been able to obtain spices, herbs, oils, silks, linens, velvet even by trading with pilgrims. Most of his trading had been small deals involving doves, or olive oil, but occasionally he was able to trade or sell one of his sheep or arrange the sale of livestock owned by his brothers.

His reminiscing turned to daydreaming about the small luxuries of life he enjoyed, and how he would be able to afford more of these little pleasures. He enjoyed sweet bread in the mornings. He enjoyed the honey and spices they were wealthy enough to buy from the market. It wasn't just the honey and small luxuries Abram desired. An increase in business meant an improvement in his social status, better contacts and opportunities for his son. It meant he might find a better husband for his daughter, having put off arranging her marriage long enough. It was time to find a husband for her. She would be thirteen within the year. Time was running short to find a suitable husband. He was hoping this meeting with Caiaphas would lay the groundwork for a better future for his family. He planned to enroll Jonas in studies with the scribes. He wanted a better life for his son. He planned to find a wealthy husband for Sarah. He planned to move his family from their small village of Bethpage into Jerusalem. He dreamed of having sweet bread with honey every morning, not just a few times a month. Now these seeds of his desires were on the verge of being planted, the harvest would be an improved life among the wealthy of Jerusalem.

The donkey made its way over the rough road and Abrams thoughts returned to the present. He knew the bale of silk would be an impressive gift to Caiaphas and hoped his offer would secure his place in the Temple for all of the holy weeks. Three weeks a year all Jewish people were required to visit the Temple. When the Sanhedrin approved having merchants in the Temple area Abram was one of many to apply. The coincidence of getting moved closer to the men's entrance made him realize the advantage of location. But it also opened his eyes to expanding his business. He had to win a contract with Caiaphas to collect the Temple tax.

A pain in his side, maybe a small cramp, bothered him momentarily. Coincidentally, the memory of his initial resistance to setting up his merchant table inside the Temple entered his mind at that moment. Something about setting up his booth inside the Temple didn't seem right. Some merchants even brought cattle or sheep into the courtyard of the Temple. Doves in cages didn't seem so bad, but sheep and cattle in the courtyard of the beautiful Temple seemed out of place. People bartering, negotiating, and exchanging money in the courtyards didn't feel right, even if the animal was going to be sacrificed. The Temple is such a grand place, all gold and white, beautiful and magnificent. The God of Israel lives in the room called the Holy of Holies at the back of the Temple. But eventually Abram rationalized his doubts by thinking there was something noble, perhaps even blessed about being in the Temple selling doves for sacrifices. It was his way of serving

God. It was an honor he told himself. If this was how things were to be, then he might as well profit from it. So he finally embraced the idea of doing business inside the Temple. There could really be nothing wrong with it, and if the Sanhedrin approved, who was he to argue?

So today he would offer Caiaphas his gifts, and if necessary, a small portion of his profits for the stall closest to the men's entry during festival weeks. He would only bring up the subject today, but hoped he would also be awarded a contract to collect the Temple tax. The Temple tax had provided the High Priests with a fine life and Abram saw a way for it to improve his own life. He didn't agree with doing business in the Temple, but if it were to be, then he wanted to be the first merchant men would see. His stall would be the busiest and all his hopes and dreams could start to come true.

Abram crested a small hill and the city of Jerusalem laid spread out before him a short distance away, the Temple gleamed brightly. He was to meet Malchus at the Gate of Gentiles and be escorted to his meeting with Caiaphas. He prodded the donkey on, heading down the final stretch toward the Temple. It was beautiful.

I finished mucking the stall and brought some barley hay out front to feed the colt and ass. I tied them next to a fig tree by the entry into our courtyard. Mother and Sarah were already grinding barley grain into flour to make bread. I knew I was expected to help since they would be baking more bread than usual in case any hungry pilgrims approached seeking food and a campsite. That wasn't so unusual during the festive weeks when pilgrims traveled to Jerusalem. For a small fee, Father would allow pilgrims to camp on part of our property, though many times bartering replaced the exchange of any money. The festival of Passach or Passover is next week and we have already had a number of pilgrims passing by this week. Some of them are camping on our property already. Jerusalem city limits have been expanded this week all the way up to our property. They do this to accommodate the law that requires all Jews to be in Jerusalem city limits during the holy week.

The colt nudged my hand as I brought the hay for them to feed on. They'd usually spend the hours of their day lazing in the shade; in the small area fenced in by our courtyard. They seemed more like pets than working animals, but the mule did help turn the olive press. I wondered why Father suggested I tie them in front of our house but did as I was told. Then I went to help mother and Sarah bake the bread before I left for Bethpage to study at the synagogue. But within minutes of tying the animals out front, two men approached the mule and its foal, untied them and started leading them away. I cried out, running toward them shouting for them to stop. "Why do you loose our colt?" they turned around and replied "The Lord hath need of them." Without knowing why, without understanding, I knew it would be all right. I didn't know what I'd tell Father, but I knew it was meant to be. I wouldn't have to worry about how we'd get the animals back. The words "Our Lord hath need of them." echoed in my ears as I watched them lead the animals up the road toward Bethany.

The rest of that day was uneventful. I finished my chores and went into Bethpage to begin my afternoon studies of the Torah. I didn't know what I would tell Father about the ass and colt and hoped he would be too busy with pilgrims to become angry over letting two men take our animals. Two strangers walking down the road from Bethany is not an unusual sight this time of year; pilgrims on their way to the Temple. But pilgrims don't usually take your livestock unless they're thieves. The road in front of our house is well traveled, and I hoped those men were pilgrims and not thieves. If the Lord needs our ass and colt, surely he would be traveling to the Temple as well. I would watch the road these coming days, and reclaim our animals after this "Lord" has finished using them. I wondered what they meant by "Our Lord had need of them." Who was it these men called Lord? Could they be talking about Jesus of Nazareth? All of Jerusalem knew about Jesus. Some say he is The Christ. He's a friend of Lazarus from Bethany and raised him from the dead late last year; raised him from the dead. I thought about that for a moment. It created quite a commotion locally. People traveled from Jerusalem to Bethany just to see Lazarus. I've never seen so many people traveling the road from Jerusalem to Bethany unless it was the end of a holy week. They returned to their synagogues talking about how Jesus of Nazareth had raised Lazarus from death but this just caused more people to go and see Lazarus for themselves. The priests didn't seem to believe any of this until they visited Lazarus too. Then they didn't trust his newfound popularity and tried to find a reason to have him arrested.

I heard other stories about Jesus. He was getting to be well known around Jerusalem over the past couple of years. Last year at Passover, Roman authorities had gone around asking people if they knew of any laws Jesus might have broken. Don't ask me why. Jesus had been staying with Lazarus; and his sisters Martha and Mary.

Lazarus had become a local legend. He died late last year. He did die. I remember Mother went to their home to be a "wailer" for his funeral. Mother knew Martha and Mary through the synagogue, so she volunteered to help. That was a custom, the women of the villages, friends, or relatives would move as a group in a funeral procession crying and wailing as they walked to the gravesite. Men waited at the gravesite singing praise to God for the life and blessings of the deceased while they were alive. I remember Mother said the sisters were very upset over the death of their brother. They sent for Jesus while Lazarus was ill, but he arrived after Lazarus died. Then I started hearing the same story from different people of Bethany, Jesus had the stone in front of the grave rolled away, raised his eyes to the sky, stretched out his arms and called out *"Lazarus, rise!"* And he did! Lazarus had been dead for four days! The smell must have been awful. People heard about it and descended on Bethany and the home of Lazarus. Yes, Lazarus was a real local legend.

So, if this 'Lord' was Jesus, then he'd be going to the Temple this week. I'll keep watch over the road and get Sarah to help. They'll have to pass this way. We'll get our animals back. Father won't be angry with me.

Abram approached Malchus on entering the gate of Gentiles; the entry for men. He was attending to the duties involved with collecting the Temple tax from visitors. "Good morning Malchus, Shalom. It's a fine day. I hope you're doing well." Abram spoke, approaching the liaison to the High Priest. Malchus smiled at Abram offering his hand in a Roman gesture of greeting.

"Yes thank you. But I have better things to do than stay here collecting the tax. You'll be having a good day my friend. May I suggest we talk before our meeting with Caiaphas? I'd like to review the details of our arrangement." He turned to another servant at the table and said; "I must find Caiaphas, count the currency twice and record the details. Don't make any mistakes or you'll have trouble. Do this well, and you'll be rewarded." He motioned for Abram to follow him. The two walked into the courtyard toward the Temple itself. "You see Abram; it is a matter of supervision. There're only a handful of servants that can help do the work. They can read, write, and count. They're trustworthy and honest but require supervision. So you'll have a servant to help you sell your doves. Their compensation comes from the taxes. Caiaphas wanted me to make sure you understood that before meeting with him. He needs someone to focus on collecting the tax. There're so many pilgrims from different countries, he needs someone that knows how to make change." Abram smiled at the prospect of this opportunity so neatly falling into alignment with his plan. It seemed his desire and the needs of Caiaphas were not that different. They approached the door to the council room of the Temple. Before entering, Abram reached into his small bag of coins and gave one to Malchus. "I wanted to thank you for making this meeting happen. I know this arrangement will help you perform your duties for the High Priest, and help my business. I think we'll work very well together." Malchus took the piece of silver saying "Thank you, but be warned; don't cross Caiaphas. It's best to stay on his good side." With that, he opened the council door and led Abram to Caiaphas sitting behind a small table reading what appeared to be a letter of complaint.

Thursday Evening

Father was angry. He couldn't understand how I could just let strangers take our animals. He reprimanded me not trying to stop the strangers, like I could have stopped those two men myself. So he encouraged me to watch over the road Friday that we might be able to regain our animals. He went on about me becoming a responsible grown man throughout dinner; how I'd better learn to make wiser decisions. Mother was more forgiving since she believed that it was indeed Jesus who needed the animals. She and the other women of the village talked about Jesus and the things they had heard. She marveled at the stories of his miracles; making the blind see, the deaf hear. And of course, there was Lazarus. She knows the family and has seen Lazarus since his "rebirth". So Mother wasn't at all concerned about the animals and only hoped it was Jesus who needed them.

"Perhaps Jesus would even bless our home with a visit and have a meal with us. Surely we could offer him comfort and respite for a brief time and learn from him."

When mother said this, Father held his tongue, but I could tell he was still angry with me. Later, away from Father, Mother hugged me and said things would work out, that I should not worry.

I felt relieved.

Friday

The sun rose slowly over the eastern horizon. The sky was a crisp light blue and the air felt cool as it breathed over the skin moving eastward toward Jerusalem. I had just helped Father load the cages of doves and pigeons on the donkey to make the journey to the Temple. Abram reached out putting his hand on my shoulder.

"Jonas, I'm sorry for getting angry yesterday. Keep watch over the road this morning, perhaps you'll see the animals. Get them back if you do. If this 'Lord' is an honest man; you'll have no problems. I'll be at Temple until evening prayers are finished. God has blessed us! I have the first table entering the court of Gentiles and begin collecting the Temple tax today for the High Council. What do you think of that? You Father is on the path to success. But it means I'll be staying late. Go to synagogue for your studies this afternoon, and help your sister and mother bake extra bread. There're many pilgrims this week." He swatted the donkey to start the trek to Jerusalem.

I was off to muck the stall in back of our house. I finished sooner than normal since there were two less animals to clean up after. It was still well before the noon hour when I heard the cries of men and women coming down the road from Bethany. At first I couldn't make out what they were yelling but as they approached, the sounds became clearer. "Hosanna, Hosanna!" And "Blessed is he that cometh in the name of the Lord!" Could this be the 'Lord' that needed our ass and colt? How lucky. I *knew* it would work out, I'd be able to get our animals back and Father would forgive my transgression. This 'Lord' is coming down the road to Jerusalem, what luck. And if I couldn't get the animals now, I could follow and bring them back after their missive was complete. I ran to the front of our house and joined Sarah and mother as we watched the gathering approach.

Indeed there was a man riding side-saddle on the back of our ass. Our young colt walked alongside, carrying on his back folded bundles of cloth, perhaps a tent for shelter. All around this man were at least twenty other people, some of them strangers and obviously pilgrims. This had to be the one they called "Lord." The men were all singing "Hosanna! Hosanna!" as they came down the road. There were villagers from Bethany walking with this group too. I recognized some of them. A small crowd of people was moving down the road to Jerusalem and I had a feeling I would soon be following them with Sarah simply out of curiosity. We would both be able to skip the remainder of our chores if that really was Jesus. Father would approve because now I could get our animals back. Mother would let us follow the small crowd just because it was Jesus.

I saw the family of Simon the Leper, and then I saw Simon himself. He was also well known as one of the local miracles Jesus performed. He looked healthy, without a blemish or any of his skin peeling off. Lazarus was walking alongside Jesus sitting on the ass, Martha and Mary followed close behind. They were all singing "Hosanna" and "Blessed be the kingdom of our Father, David, that cometh in the name of the Lord: Hosanna in the highest."

Some of the men, maybe followers of Jesus, would start a chant of "Hosanna! Hosanna!" And all of the travelers would respond equally as enthusiastically in a sing-song way "Hosanna! Hosanna!" Many of the people were throwing their garments down on the ground for the ass to walk on. Some were spreading palm branches down, others just waving them about as they all shouted "Hosanna, Hosanna in the highest!" There seemed to be a celebration moving down the road to Jerusalem.

I stood there with mother and Sarah watching the parade of villagers and this mysterious man, Jesus, if that really was him, moving down the road to Jerusalem. "Can we follow?" I asked mother. "Sarah and I will be careful, and we'll be able to bring back the ass and colt." I wasn't begging her yet, but I didn't look forward to practicing my writing at the synagogue later. I wanted to follow this group of people raising their voices in praise. Maybe I would see a miracle for myself. Jesus has supposedly cured many sick people that come to him. There're stories about him feeding thousands of people on a couple of loaves of bread and a few fish. That's crazy talk to some people. Father has more than once questioned whether the people telling these stories were just spreading gossip and rumors; reminding me at the same time that it's a sin to spread rumors. He'd say "Most of those people were not there to witness thousands being fed, and on just a few loaves of bread and fish! I have no reason to believe they would lie to me, Jonas, I just don't know if they are truthful." Mother would marvel at the stories and say this man must surely be a prophet since he taught in the Temples and cured the sick. Maybe he would be the one to help the Jewish people with the authorities of Rome. Maybe he was the Messiah that would unite the Jewish nation and conquer our oppressors, Rome.

There's reason to believe all these rumors around Bethpage. There's Simon the Leper, and Lazarus the resurrected; both from Bethany. Now they're two local legends and friends of Jesus. Only once did I see Simon when he was diseased. I was young, about four years ago. We went to the Temple during Passover week and I remember thinking the road to Jerusalem was dusty, long and hilly. Sarah and I saw Simon the Leper on the side of the road begging for alms right outside the city. I remember seeing the red blotches on the bits of skin he wasn't able to keep covered. Like they were open sore that wouldn't heal. Now, there he went, walking down the road as if he'd never been diseased, singing happily and joyfully.

I didn't have to ask twice when I looked up at Mother again with my eyes pleading to allow us to follow this crowd while it was still passing by our house. "We'll bring back the ass and colt before sundown, I promise mother, please?" She told me to gather a water flask, stay with Sarah always, and be respectful of the people we meet. Sarah and I would join in with all the followers on the road to Jerusalem and return later with the animals. I ran into the house to get the goatskin water flask.

The trek to Jerusalem was wonderful, nothing like the way I remembered! Sarah and I skipped and danced more than walked along the road with these travelers. The road didn't seem as long or dusty this time. The men walking with Jesus were friendly and happy. A man in ragged clothing was walking alongside, but his clothes didn't seem to matter to anyone and he was part of this group. Next to him was a politician, the chief publican Zacchaeus. It looked pretty odd, the rich politician walking next to the beggar in ragged clothes. Zacchaeus wasn't very popular either from the way I heard Father speak about him. He looked out of place alongside Simon the Leper and Lazarus the resurrected. But all of them joined in singing praise and raising their voices in joy as they walked down the road. It even seemed Zacchaeus sang the loudest.

This group of people walking to Jerusalem grew with every turn of the road. Pilgrims camping out or resting on the roadside joined us and soon a small parade was making its way to the Temple. Sarah and I trailed along near the back of the group taking in the sight and sounds. Then a man started talking to us, a man in a tattered tunic, a beggar really. He told Sarah and I a story of being blind just last week. He'd been born blind and had never seen the light of day. His name was Bartimaeus and he followed Jesus here from Jericho. He said he was begging on the side of the road in Jericho for scraps of food, or a penny or two when he heard a crowd of people approaching. He asked 'Who's in this crowd of people?' and 'Who's causing such a commotion on the road from Jericho?' Someone told him it was the prophet Jesus of Nazareth. "When I heard this I cried out as loudly as I could 'Jesus, thou son of David, have mercy on me!' I yelled it again, and again. Then someone smacked me on the side of my head, told me to be still, and hold my peace. Hold my peace, as if I could! I cried out louder 'Jesus, thou son of David Have mercy on me' again and again."

"What happened next?" Sarah asked, amazed by this beggar man and his jubilation over following Jesus.

"What happened next? What happened next? I'll tell you what happened next. Jesus asked me "What would I have Him do for me?" So I told him I was blind from birth and wanted sight more than anything." The beggar looked down at us, staring up in amazement. He smiled at us with his new-born eyes. "Jesus said to me; 'receive thy sight: thy faith hath saved thee." And by the act of God I saw. I saw with my own eyes for the first time in my life. I saw and I cried. This man is from God. This man is holy. He healed me. I was blind but now I see!" He looked ahead at Jesus on the mule, raised his hands in the air and cried

"Hosanna, I can see because of that man. Hosanna to the son of David!" Then he ran on ahead singing out "Hosanna! Hosanna!" in response to all of the disciples starting up another song of praise.

Sarah and I stopped walking and stared at each other in amazement and disbelief. We'd just met someone that was touched by Jesus. We just met one of his miracles. The stories we heard had to be true. We just spoke with someone who said he was born blind! He saw for the first time in his life just last week. Just because Jesus told him he could see and he believed it. I grabbed Sarah's hand and we ran up ahead to strip some palm fronds from the trees like other people were doing to spread them on the ground for the procession. We walked, danced, sang on the way to the Temple.

And we talked with some of the men following Jesus. They called themselves disciples and said they had been traveling with Jesus for about three years. Some of the men had been fishermen casting nets in the waters off Galilee. They all had jobs they quit just to follow Jesus, and they carried no material wealth with them when they traveled. In fact they gave up all they owned to follow Jesus. I asked how they survived, how they ate from day to day and slept. They said all their worldly worries seemed small when they were around Jesus. They never lacked for anything; never went hungry. They were usually spared the elements of nature because some family would open their stable or barn for the men to sleep in if it rained. They had tents but people would offer to feed or house them after hearing Jesus teach in the Temple. They marveled at his wisdom as he spoke to crowds and taught.

We learned some of their names and they said that Jesus gave them each a new name. One of them called Simon

Peter used to be called Saul. He was talkative and friendly. We met another named James. And another who was not as friendly. His name was Judas and he almost seemed out of place. He was with them, but seemed removed in some way too. He wasn't as jubilant when singing "Hosanna". Simon Peter said he was the treasurer of the group. He laughed and said Judas was often too worried about our worldly needs, where they would get their next meal or shelter, rather than learning from Jesus all the spiritual things there were to know. I was walking close enough to hear a Pharisee ask Jesus if he thought it wise to be shouting Hosanna and singing so loudly, to which Jesus replied *"I tell you, if they keep quiet, the stones will cry out."* I wondered what that would sound like; to hear rocks and stones shout out 'Hosanna' and laughed to myself as I joined in singing with the others.

But I swear the air was full of sound. And it did indeed sound like rocks and trees all around us were singing too.

People continued to join the group as we made our way to the Temple. Singing filled the air, though not by any of the Pharisees that started following in Bethpage. They eyed Jesus and all of us rather suspiciously I thought, but what did I know, a boy of twelve. I knew they were Pharisees though having seen them at the synagogue. It was late afternoon when we entered the walls of Jerusalem following Jesus to the very bottom of a stairway to the Temple. Jesus looked at me as I held the reins of the donkey while he hopped down.

"Are these your animals, my child?"

"Yes rabbi."

"And your name?"

"Jonas, rabbi."

"Well then, thank you Jonas, for allowing me to use them. They've served me well and helped fulfill the words of the prophet Isaiah."

I watched as he washed his feet, hands and face in the bath at the bottom of the steps and climbed the procession of stairs up through the Gate of the Gentiles. The crowd followed. Sarah stayed with the ass and colt since she wasn't allowed in this entry anyway. She waited at the bottom of the stairs as I went up to try to find Father and tell him we retrieved our animals. I blended in with the crowd of men climbing the stairs behind Jesus, afraid that I might be scolded. I'm not old enough yet to use this entrance. But no one paid attention to me as all eyes were on Jesus. He slowed down his pace, looked around at all the merchants, my Fathers' table now being the first one upon entering the gateway. Jesus said nothing.

I quietly made my way over to Father who was busy making change for some foreign currency.

"Jonas! What are you doing here? Does your mother know you're here?" Father exclaimed as he saw me. He noticed the group of men entering the Temple but I'm not sure he saw Jesus.

"I've found our colt and ass Father! Sarah is with them down the stairs, see!" I exclaimed. Abram took a step outside, looked down to see Sarah holding rein over the donkey and young foal. "And the Lord those men spoke of was that man Jesus of Nazareth. See, he's just entered the courtyard. We followed him here after he passed by our house this morning. There were lots of people on the way too! Look at all the villagers that followed him here! We were singing Hosanna and waving palm branches." I could hardly contain my excitement. Father noticed, put his hand on my shoulder and started walking down the steps with me by his side.

"Yes, this is good Jonas, and I'm sure you stayed with your sister at all times on the way here?"

"Yes, Father, and we were with villagers from Bethpage as well, Lazarus and his sisters were there."

"Yes well, I guess there's some comfort in that thought, They've been blessed. Very well then, the animals are in good health, yes?"

"Yes, Father."

"Then make way home with your sister. Let her ride the donkey and don't dally. I want you to be home before the sun sets."

"Yes, Father," I set off down the stairs to Sarah and the animals. We talked about everything we heard on the journey earlier that day; all the people walking along, everyone singing 'Hosanna'.

Saturday

"It's not right. You should not be working today Abram. It's against the law of God. Nothing good can come of it." Mother was speaking to Father, nervously moving around the small area of the house that was used as a dining space. Sarah and I sat cross- legged picking at the fruit and bread before us watching mother nervously move around the room, acting like she was cleaning. "You *must* not go today Abram. You simply must not go; you know how disobedience of God's law will bring suffering."

"Elizabeth, don't worry. It's been approved by the Sanhedrin. The Sadducees themselves presented the offer to all the Jewish merchants. You are sounding like a Sadducee yourself, worrying too much about the letter of the law. Is it not a law to Honor God? I'm simply helping others honor God. Besides, I have secured the entry table! Business will be much better; we should be able to do very well. Don't you want to move to Jerusalem? We'll have a better life once we're able to do that. I've been able to win the favor of Caiaphas, no easy task that was. Just being able to do business with the priests of the Temple should be profitable. They enjoy such luxuries! And we will too! Once I've established myself. Don't worry that I'm working on the Sabbath, the Sanhedrin have approved and forgiven this transgression during festival weeks.

Father turned to us, "Jonas, Sarah; are you finished eating? Jonas, pray the birkat ha-mazon, then help me with the dove cages. I want you to come to the Temple after your morning chores. Today may be a good day for you to learn about foreign currencies with so many pilgrims."

I finished my figs and bread, put my plate aside and spoke clearly and slowly in Hebrew as I learned in my studies for my bar mitzvah. "Thank you God for this food you have provided for us. Thank you for the food you give the world. Thank you God for bringing us forth from the land of Egypt, establishing your covenant with the Jewish people, and for the promise of the land of Israel as our inheritance." Father looked at me, nodded his head and smiled. I headed out the door to the stables in our courtyard.

I was strapping the dove cages to the back of the donkey as Father strode up carrying a bundle of fine cloth and box of small bottles of olive oil. "Jonas, feed the other animals and muck their stall before you come to the Temple. We have enough flour for your mother and sister to bake the bread; they won't need your help today. Bring your writing tablet to practice, a good businessman will usually stay busy, but there can be times that are slow, it's wise for you to keep your mind active during the idle times."

"Father, are you sure the High Priest can forgive breaking a mitzvoth d'oraita?"

I had always known to keep the Sabbath holy and that Jews believed it was to be a day of rest and prayer honoring the one true God, but I was trying to show off some of the knowledge I learned while studying the Torah for my bar mitzvah. A mitzvoth is like a law or commandment, d'oraita meant this law came from the Torah rather than laws by Rabbis. There're 613 laws that are mitzvot d'oraita, from the Torah. Some of them are clear, explicit commands in the text. I was bothered that Father was going to work on the Sabbath, clearly against the written word.

"It's good that you ask this question, Jonas. It shows you're beginning to think as a man. But the Sanhedrin is the highest authority of the Jewish people and they have given permission for merchants to be in the Temple. It's a busy week ahead and there are many pilgrims. The Temple tax must be collected, and sacrifices must be made. There's a need now because it's Passover week. We'll only be in the Temple 'til Wednesday, and we'll leave well before sundown to celebrate the Seder meal. Now go finish your chores. I expect to see you later this morning, before noon." With that he swatted the donkey and started down the road to Jerusalem.

I finished my chores, wrapped some bread and figs in a small linen bindle with my writing tablet and began my trek to the Temple. The road was again busy with pilgrims and local villagers heading toward Jerusalem for Sabbath services. I fell in behind a family I recognized from Bethpage, preferring to walk on the outside of a small group rather than by myself. As the city came into view, the Temple shone white and gold on the horizon. Many of the pilgrims broke into song proclaiming the glory of God and being rescued from slavery by the Egyptians. It was a little different from our trek yesterday. There was a joy in their voice as they sang and I joined them, but the air wasn't filled with sound like it was yesterday.

I washed my feet in the bath at the bottom of the steps toward the Gate of the Gentiles; Father said I would find him directly inside this entrance where all the men entered the Temple. I hesitated climbing the stairs again, since I was not yet considered a man, but made my way up to the entry and immediately saw my Father collecting the Temple tax from someone. He had one of the High Priests servants helping him sell the doves. Walking toward the table, Father greeted me with a big smile and open arms. "I hope you've brought some extra bread for our new friend helping me today. Pretty soon, you will be able to sit here with me and sell the doves as I collect the Temple tax. What do you think of that? Helping your Father in his business; learning the tools of the trade. And when we move to Jerusalem you'll be able to study with the scribes. I've already spoken with the High Priest Caiaphas about you studying with the scribes."

I didn't reply but wasn't too thrilled about the prospect of having to study with the scribes. I enjoyed practicing my writing and was glad I had learned to read. I even helped Sarah learn to read some, but girls are not supposed to waste their time doing those kinds of things. They're supposed to grind the flour, bake the bread; prepare the meals.

"That'd be great, Father." I said without much enthusiasm. "Is there something I can do to help?" I asked really just wanting to find a place to sit and watch everyone here at the Temple. I was hoping I could walk around a little, maybe stand in the entryway of the Great Courtyard where the sacrifices were made by the priests and watch.

"Not now." Father replied, "I want you to stay close by though, I don't want to have to go looking for you when I'm ready to leave. We'll be going to Sabbath services this evening, your mother and sister will meet us at the synagogue in Bethpage."

"Yes, Father, I'll stay close and practice my writing. But can I go watch the priest offer sacrifices." With his permission, I set off a short way down the grand corridor finding a spot between the massive columns where I could see into the Great

Courtyard and the altar where the sacrifices were made. People milled about, in a line waiting to give the priest their dove. A few people brought an old goat, but most offered the common dove bought from a merchant like my Father or from their own home. I pulled out my wax tablet and started practicing writing the alphabet and simple words since I didn't have a Torah with me to copy. From my spot between the columns, I was virtually hidden from view, though I could simply look around the side of the column and see the entrance and Father at his table. It was late morning before noon when I sensed something different about the day. The wind had stopped; you could hear the birds singing, not just a few here and there. No, the sounds of the birds singing filled the air in a way I had never heard before. I looked around the column to see a group of men enter the Gate of the Gentiles. I recognized Jesus right away. Next to him was Simon Peter who Sarah and I spoke with yesterday morning. There were the other men that had walked the road with us from Bethpage to Jerusalem. They were his disciples, the ones who stayed with him traveling around from village to village. But Jesus had a stern look on his face; he seemed to be scowling, or maybe it seemed to be a pained expression as he stopped a short way into the Temple colonnade. He stood looking at my Father for what seemed like a minute, but also was taking view of the other merchants in the colonnade as well. I couldn't take my eyes off him.

What happened next shocked me, stunned Father, and silenced the crowd of people milling about. He strode over to Fathers table, the first upon entering the great gate, grabbed it and flung it across the colonnade floor. Then, he moved determinedly to the next closest table, and the next, turning them over, flinging dove cages to the floor, until he had come full circle inside the entryway. Standing in the center of the colonnade he looked around at all the stunned faces of the merchants, my Father, mouth open eyes wide, staring. Jesus finally spoke loudly and with authority; *"Is it not written, 'My house shall be called of all nations the house of prayer?' But you have made it a den of thieves."* He slowly walked toward the great courtyard as my Father and the other merchants bent to pick up their table and strewn belongings. All the people standing about followed, murmuring to themselves and each other about what just happened. A man walking with a severe limp, dragging his left leg, shuffled over to Jesus; fell to his knees bowing. I couldn't hear what was said between them but I saw the man rise and walk away without a limp. I looked over at Father who hadn't taken his eyes off the man that just turned his life upside down. Intently staring in amazement, or bafflement, he watched the lame man walk away too. Father just stood there with his money bag in hand, staring at the crowd of people gathering around Jesus. It was as if he didn't know what to do, which way to turn, so he just kept watching. He didn't continue his business. He didn't stop pilgrims to remind them to pay their tax; he didn't offer anyone a dove for sacrificing. He stood spellbound and confused as to whether to continue the business of the day, or pack everything up and leave the most profitable location in all of Jerusalem to make his living.

Caiaphas strode up to Father at that moment, quickly, as if he had rushed here to handle the situation that happened five minutes earlier. "Abram, are you hurt? That man was Jesus of Nazareth, has he harmed you?"

"No, no. I'm well. But I'm not sure what to do next. What he said, that we are making his house into a den of thieves, *his* house?"

"He said *his* house?" Caiaphas asked.

"Yes. What do you think he meant by that?" But Caiaphas had already turned away and called to Malchus. They spoke briefly, and Caiaphas, seeing other priests and Pharisees standing together; broke away from Malchus and strode toward them.

Malchus turned to Father, "Abram, sir, Caiaphas has asked me to assist you in collecting the Temple tax, if you wish, and not to be deterred by the words of the Nazarene. Everything can return to normal now."

"He seemed really angry that we're doing business here in the Temple." Father replied.

"Sir, Caiaphas assures me, he is nothing more than a rebel to the Jewish laws, and his so called miracles are the works of a magician. Perhaps he is possessed. Caiaphas says he can't be trusted, so I don't trust him."

Father slowly moved to his position and quietly returned to serving the pilgrims entering the Temple.

I returned to watching Jesus talking with and healing the pilgrims that approached him. I was trying to scratch a few letters on the wax tablet, but was transfixed by watching the crowd in front of me. Then I heard the grumblings of some Sadducees that had come to stand near the column I was resting against. I peeked around and saw Caiaphas among a group of five.

"This man Jesus is dangerous. See how the people flock to him." one said.

"His influence over them is growing." Another

responded. "We must find a way to discredit him. Make the people question his teachings."

"We need to find a way to arrest him." Caiaphas replied coldly. "He's becoming too popular. We failed last year; we must not fail this year."

"Yes," said another, "and the sooner the better."

Caiaphas replied "We can't do it before the Passover feast. He's too popular; it would be a disturbance to holy week and may cause more trouble than it's worth. We need to wait until the end of the week. Then we need to find a way to bring him before the Sanhedrin, after the Passover feast. We must stay alert to his words and question his teachings whenever possible. We must find a way to trap him so we can legitimize his arrest before the people. Stay alert I say. Question him when you can, in front of everyone. Surely he'll give us some reason to arrest him. Then he'll lose favor with the people and our task will be easy."

Quickly I turned my body back to my side of the column for fear of being seen. I couldn't understand why the chief priest here at the Temple didn't like Jesus. I couldn't see anything but sick people being healed. Now, women and children gathered about him saying 'Hosanna to the Son of David' and asking for a blessing. No reason to arrest him, unless it was for turning over tables and making a mess in the Temple. What he said about making Gods' house into a den of thieves made sense to me. I didn't think the merchants should be in the Temple at all. I held my breath as I waited for the group of priests to move on so I could leave my hiding place. Jesus stood and started walking our way as if to leave the Temple. The crowd of people, women and children followed him, some still saying 'Hosanna to the Son of David!" Hearing this again, Caiaphas approached him slowly with his group of Sadducees following. Maybe he was just trying to avert another table tossing as Jesus left the Temple, but he said to Jesus, "Do you think it wise that the children call you the Son of David?"

To which I heard Jesus reply *"Yea; have ye never read, 'Out of the mouth of babes and suckling's thou hast perfected praise?'"* Then he walked on past the Sadducees, looking at the merchants as he left, lingering on my Fathers eyes for what seemed like a very long moment as he passed by.

Father and I packed the mule with the empty dove cages, tablecloth and floor mat in the late afternoon to reach the synagogue in Bethpage before sundown. We attended Sabbath and made it home before sunset. Father was exceptionally quiet the rest of the evening. During supper I tried to tell Sarah what I had seen, the lame man walking away; all the women and children singing 'Hosanna' like we did on our way to Jerusalem yesterday. But whenever I started to speak, Father would just look at me and frown a little, as if it'd be better for me to stay silent. I kept thinking about Caiaphas wanting to arrest Jesus and wondered how the priests of the Temple and our faith could be against someone that seemed to be so good.

Sunday

Father remained in a quiet mood this morning. So I told him I was looking forward to going to the Temple with him. It wasn't because I wanted to learn my Father's trade. I knew Jesus would be teaching at the Temple. Somehow I knew Jesus would be there every day while he was in Jerusalem. The people would hardly leave him alone, and he seemed to care so much about teaching them and healing the sick. I was sure he would be at the Temple. I was hoping Father would again let me join the crowds rather than work, so I could hear and learn from this prophet.

We arrived and washed our feet in the bath before climbing the steps leading to the entry. There were Roman guards stationed just inside, four of them stationed as you entered each of the four gates to the Temple. Their stern glances touched on all the pilgrims entering, perhaps looking for; waiting for Jesus to turn over some more tables and arrest him. Caiaphas said he didn't want Jesus arrested before Passover feast but I bet he wouldn't mind arresting Jesus if he thought he had a good reason.

Maybe I could warn Jesus between now and then. Maybe I could help him avoid getting arrested. I mean, if he gave the Sanhedrin no reason, then they couldn't arrest him could they? Once our table was set up and I arranged the dove cages, Father had me practice my counting using his bag of half-shekels. He wanted me to stay and help sell the doves, but saw the look of disappointment on my face knowing I wanted to go listen to Jesus. "Don't worry, Jonas, you'll be able to learn from the prophet today. I saw that lame man walk away. I'm having second thoughts about being here in the Temple; selling doves; collecting the tax for Caiaphas. No matter how profitable it may be. We're living well, no? You're doing well studying at the synagogue in Bethpage, right? Perhaps this will be the last festival we work here. Perhaps." His voice trailed off quietly. He seemed to be talking more to himself than to me now, as if he were lost in thought, trying to piece together loosely connected ideas.

Malchus strode up followed by two servants. "Good morning Abram, it's good to see you. Caiaphas wanted me to assure you there won't be any more disturbances. You see? We have asked the Roman authorities for guards to be stationed at the Temple gates."

"Good morning Malchus. Yes. I see the guards but I can tell you I'm not happy about having these pagans inside the Temple colonnade, so close to the Temple itself, even if they are here to protect me."

"It will only be during Passover week. This so called 'prophet' Jesus has stirred the hearts of all the people with his magic. I can tell you in confidence that he is being watched closely. He won't cause any more trouble. Caiaphas is expecting a record number of pilgrims, and has provided you two servants with knowledge of counting. They can be trusted to assist you with the doves. But it's important to keep the people moving and collect the tax."

"Yes, yes. Thank you very much. They'll be of great assistance. Pass my gratitude on to Caiaphas. I won't let a pilgrim pass without asking for the tax."

Father started teaching me about different currencies and how to exchange foreign dinars or shekels into the Tyrian shekel, which was required to pay the Temple tax. The Tyrian shekel was made from the finest silver and accepted everywhere. I looked over at the Roman guards every now and then wondering what these men really thought about our Jewish people coming to the Temple in droves each year to pay homage to our one true God. Rome conquered us years ago, long before I was born. But they allow us to practice our own religion instead of paying homage to their pagan gods. They just take a share of all our money and crops. Three times a year during our religious festivals, troops of roman guards descend upon Jerusalem, doubling the number of men normally stationed here. Maybe they're scared of having so many Jews gathered in one city at one time. This year it seemed there were even more guards than before. I heard Pontius Pilate, the Roman procurator, had come all the way from Rome to Jerusalem this year, and with him more troops of Roman pagans. I wondered if he had heard about Jesus turning over the tables. I guess he could pass judgment and settle any disturbances for Rome while he was here. Pilate wasn't liked by us Jews. Father said he wasn't really Jewish, that he couldn't have been after he tried to "line the streets of Jerusalem with pagan Roman images". This caused a small riot by the people of Jerusalem. And then there was the fact he stole from the Temple treasury to build the aqueduct for his palace. No one in Jerusalem thought very highly of Pontius Pilate. Well, no Jew.

Caiaphas' servants took over handling the doves. Father managed the money changing and I practiced writing on my wax tablet unless Father asked me to record an exchange in his ledger or add up some ledger entries to practice my counting. Then he'd make me figure out how much our share was for doing the exchange. He was insistent on my learning to read, write and count. He said 'the path to success was knowledge' but all too often I felt pressured in my studies. He kept suggesting that I aspire to become a scribe for the Temple rather than follow in his footsteps. I enjoyed writing. Maybe Father was right and I should set my goals on becoming a scribe. Then I had the brilliant idea that I would write down something I heard Jesus say when he came to teach. And I thought about how Jesus tells stories and wondered if I would be able to remember what he said, or get it written down on my writing tablet. Lost in my own thoughts, I was brought back to reality when I heard a group of men walking toward the stairs to the entry. It was Jesus and his followers, his disciples. They were washing their feet, hands and face in the bath at the bottom of the steps. I wondered what he might do when he saw the merchant tables set up again. The guards didn't move. They didn't know it was Jesus approaching, though it was because of him they were stationed here.

Jesus entered the Temple, walking slowly by our table looking at Father, but without any real expression of anger, and certainly not turning anything over or throwing dove cages to the floor.

He stopped, looked at me and to my astonishment greeted me saying *"Good morning, Jonas. I see you're practicing your writing from the Torah. I'm sure one day you will write something important."*

"Thank you, rabbi." I replied a little tongue tied and dumbstruck not knowing what to say. How did he know I had written words from the Torah on my tablet? Surely he couldn't see what I'd written. The guards eyed him constantly, ever ready to grab him over any perceived wrong-doing. I'm sure Caiaphas told them not to hesitate to arrest him should he do anything wrong.

Jesus walked on into the great courtyard where many people were gathered to watch the ritual of sacrificing doves. A crowd of people gathered around him, standing, or sitting close by asking Jesus to teach them about the law of the Jewish religion. One of the guards left his post walking down the corridor to the council room where Caiaphas sat with other priests. I looked up at Father, "May I go sit and learn from the Rabbi Father? I mean Jesus, he talks as if he's a rabbi, he teaches everyone, anyway. Maybe I'll see a miracle of healing. Please?" Father nodded his assent and I walked across the expansive aisle to my place between the columns that divided the great courtyard from the grand colonnade. Jesus was a mere twenty feet away and I could hear everything he was saying to the crowd around him. It was then that I saw Caiaphas and a number of other men approach Jesus. Among them were High Priests, elders and the scribes of the Temple with whom I might soon be studying. They had a stern look on their faces, I guess they were still angry over yesterday when Jesus turned the tables upside down and said they were a den of thieves.

Caiaphas was the first to interrupt Jesus as he was teaching the crowd of people. "Tell us, Jesus of Nazareth. By what authority do you teach? By what authority do you come into the Temple, turn over tables; and call our fine people thieves? Who might he be, that has given you such authority?"

And Jesus, in answering, said *"I will also ask of you one question, answer me and I will tell you by what authority I do these things."*

"Go on." Caiaphas replied.

"The baptism of John, was it from heaven, or of man?

Answer me and I will tell you by whose authority I do all these things."

I knew John the Baptist was a prophet. All the Jewish people revered him, and it was well known John baptized Jesus in the river Jordan some three years ago. The rumor spread that a voice from heaven sounded out after Jesus was baptized saying 'This is my beloved son, in whom I am well pleased.' This was the beginning of the legend of Jesus. Later, John the Baptist was put in prison by King Herod Antipas. Something he said about the King being a sinner because he took the wife of his half-brother. Then John's head was cut off. King Herod Antipas is not well liked by the Jewish people to say the least.

Many people were at the river Jordan being baptized by John the day he baptized Jesus. They helped spread the story of the voice everyone heard when Jesus was baptized. The next year, we started hearing stories of Jesus healing people, making blind people see, even feeding thousands of people with a few loaves of bread and fish; all sorts of amazing stories about Jesus. We never knew if we could believe any of them. But last year the thing with Lazarus happened. And that was just a village away. We all knew that really happened, so I couldn't help but believe all the other amazing stories happened too. So when Jesus asked Caiaphas, the elders and the scribes, if they thought his baptism by John was from God or simply by a man, I could tell they were troubled. I already figured out from my bar mitzvah studies that if they said 'God' because Jews believe John the Baptist was a prophet; then they would have to accept Jesus and his teachings. If they said the baptism was done by just a man, they might anger all Jews by denying John the Baptist was a prophet. They huddled together in a small group talking quietly. On emerging, Caiaphas replied "We cannot tell. We do not know."

Jesus replied back to them, *"Then neither do I tell you by whose authority I do all these things."*

Caiaphas, the other High Priests, the elders and scribes among them looked crestfallen. Slowly they moved to the back of the crowd keeping a watchful eye and ear on Jesus.

Jesus began to speak to the crowd around him. I listened, intent on hearing every word. I would listen and try to remember something I could write down later. The group of priests and elders appeared very attentive as well. *"There was a man with two sons. He came to the first and said, 'Son, go to work today in my vineyard. The boy in answer said 'No, I will not.' But later repented and went to work the vineyard as told. The man went to his second son and said likewise; 'Go into the vineyard and work today.' The second son answered and said 'I will go, sir.' But he did not go. So I ask you, which of the two sons did the will of his Father?"* And many in the crowd spoke up saying the first son, even though he at first refused, he finally did go into the vineyard. And Jesus replied to all of them *"Verily I say unto you, the publicans and harlots go into the kingdom of God before you."* Looking directly at Caiaphas and the group of elders as he said the last part; Jesus continued, *"For John came unto you in the way of righteousness and you did not believe him, but the publicans and harlots believed him. And even after you had seen it, you did not repent afterward that you might believe him."* Looking over toward Caiaphas; Jesus had not taken his eyes off the group standing in the back, I could see sternness in his eyes, and a cold glare of hate staring back.

Jesus continued speaking to the crowd gathered around him, a large semi-circle of people sitting, some reclining, others standing in the back. The elders, High Priests and Caiaphas were also listening intently in the back of the group. I saw

Malchus walk up to the right of Caiaphas standing a step behind him, waiting to heed his call.

"Hear another parable: There was a landowner who planted a vineyard. He took great care in planting hedges to surround it, and dug out the area needed for a wine press. He built a tower with which to stand watch over the entire vineyard. Then he leased it out to husbandmen to care for and harvest the fruits when he went away to a far country.

When the season of the fruit drew near, the owner sent out a servant to receive from the husbandmen the fruit of the vineyard.

But the husbandmen took his servant, beat him and sent him away empty.

Again, he sent another, and at him they cast stones, wounded him in the head, and sent him away shamefully handled.

The owner, feeling vexed, sent another, and him they killed, and many others; beating some, and killing some.

Having yet therefore one son, his well-beloved, he sent him also last unto them, saying, 'Surely they will reverence my son.'

But the husbandmen said among themselves, 'This is the heir; come, let us kill him and the inheritance shall be ours.'

And they took him, killed him, and cast him out of the vineyard.

What shall therefore the lord of the vineyard do? He will come and destroy the husbandmen, and he will give the vineyard unto others.

And have ye not read this scripture, 'the stone which the builders rejected is become the head of the corner, this was the Lord's doing, and it is marvelous in our eyes'?

Therefore I say to you: the kingdom of God shall be taken from you, and given to a nation bringing forth the fruits thereof."

Again, I noticed Jesus was looking directly at the group of elders, scribes and Caiaphas, standing behind the large group of people in front of Jesus.

"And whosoever shall fall upon this stone shall be broken: but whomever this stone falls upon, will grind him to powder."

I followed the eyes of Jesus directly to Caiaphas who had now turned toward another High Priest to his left, talking quietly to each other. The scribes and elders were also talking among themselves in hushed tones, some gesturing or directly pointing toward Jesus. Their movements and talk began to look more animated, even heated, and I started to wonder if Jesus were actually talking about them being the husbandmen. As a group, they started walking around the vast semi-circle of people gathered, walking toward Jesus. Caiaphas looked angry, and at first their stride seemed deliberate and determined, but by the time they reached the outer edge of all the people, they slowed down and stopped, hesitating to do anything while the crowd of people was gathered around him.

Monday

I woke Monday morning with a sense of excitement that I might sit in my spot again, hidden between the columns of the Temple listening to the words of this prophet Jesus. I knew he'd be back. I knew he wouldn't stay away, especially during Passover week. I gathered the doves from our coop and tried to put an extra one or two in the larger cages. We would be busy raising more doves soon but it looked like we wouldn't have any problem selling all we could this festival week. I was glad my studies at the synagogue were canceled this week. I was learning more about our Jewish religion and life listening to Jesus than I had the past year copying the Torah. On the way there I asked Father about some of the things I heard.

"Father, have you ever read in the scripture that the stone the builders rejected has become the head of the corner?" I asked.

"I'm not sure Jonas. I don't recall that exact scripture. Perhaps you can ask rabbi about it when your studies resume next week. Why? Did you hear Jesus say that yesterday?"

"Yes, Father. He tells stories, but they have a point. At least I think they have a point. Sometimes I think there's more to his stories than I understand. Like about the cornerstone. He said the stone the builders rejected became the cornerstone. Then he said whoever fell on the stone was broken, and whoever the stone fell on would be ground to powder. I don't understand any of that. I don't think the elders like his stories. They seemed to get angry about one yesterday. Some of his stories talk about the way people act toward each other, lots of times it's not very nice."

"Yes, people can be cruel. What does Jesus say about these people who don't behave very nice?"

"Bad things usually happen to them."

"That's very true. It's Good's way of punishing us for our sins. As for the elders appearing angry, They've been angry with Jesus for a couple of years now it seems. Last year rabbi warned us about the sin of gossip because there were so many rumors of miracles being performed by Jesus. I guess that's why I discourage you from spreading rumors. But then Jesus brought Lazarus back to life, and everyone in Jerusalem seemed to know about it. Remember how we saw many people traveling the road to Bethany just to visit the house of Lazarus? The Sanhedrin sent Roman guards there to look for Jesus. Remember? They even knocked on our door to ask if we knew of him or had seen him traveling the road. So many people began visiting Lazarus, I think the High Priests became concerned about his popularity, and they knew Jesus was his friend. I'll need to come listen to Jesus myself. I know he's popular with all the people, and not very popular with the leaders of our Faith. Perhaps they are afraid people will start listening to Jesus more than the High Council. He's very popular. If all the stories of miracles are true; healing the sick, making the blind see; well, maybe the High Priests have something to worry about."

We continued walking, silent.

"You know Jonas, I saw an old man limp up to Jesus the other day, and walk away as if he had the legs of a young man. It was the most amazing thing I've ever seen." Abram said a short while later.

"I believe you Father."

We arrived at Temple and washed before climbing the steps toward our table at the entry. The Roman guards were back again, already standing guard even though it was still early and no pilgrims had yet arrived. I unloaded the dove cages and was joined by the two servants of Caiaphas helping Father. Malchus came by to make sure Father was content, but soon struck up a conversation about Jesus.

"Tell me Abram, sir. Have you been able to hear any of the teachings of this man Jesus? I know you're busy here at the main entry, but he speaks to the crowds not far from here. Perhaps you'have heard him speak against the laws of our faith."

"No, I can't say I've heard much of anything, nothing more than Caiaphas and the elders themselves. They're watching him, or someone is watching for them. You yourself have been among the crowd listening to his every word. You hear for yourself he teaches according to scripture and the Torah. Do you really want to know what I think? He is a wise and learned man and we would all benefit from listening to him."

Malchus retorted, "Surely, you have heard some of the outrageous things he's said. He's been the guest of many Pharisees over the past year while traveling through Judea. He's dined with them, often without washing beforehand! He said he has the power to forgive sins! Just last month it's reported he said it was easier for a camel to go through the eye of a needle than for a rich man to enter the kingdom of God."

"You and I both know a few rich men who won't see the kingdom of God." Abram quickly replied.

"Abram, sir, this is no laughing matter. Some people

have even called him The Christ. The High Priests have said they will throw anyone calling him The Christ out of the church. And this man Jesus said if anyone thirsted, they should come unto him and drink; anyone that believes in him shall have rivers of living water flowing from him. I can't understand him half the time! He speaks in riddles the way magicians do. He can't be trusted. Many people are following him since he raised that man Lazarus from death. His popularity is building and he speaks against the real leaders of the Jews. He insults both Pharisees and Sadducees. Everyone! This *man* cannot be allowed to continue coming into Temple every holy week of every year just to stir up the people. He could cause a riot. Tell me if you see or hear anything unusual, Caiaphas would be well pleased if you can assist in this matter. Perhaps your son can help. I've noticed he sits and listens to every word intently. How about it son? Have you been listening to this man Jesus teach in the Temple?"

I was surprised Malchus had even acknowledged me, quietly tending to the doves at the end of the table, trying to eavesdrop without looking obvious. But Father became slightly angry with this new direction of conversation. "My son's a good boy and will not be dragged into digging up your dirt; you'll be kind enough to leave him out of this. I'll keep my eyes and ears open because I'm contracted by the Sanhedrin to collect the Temple tax. But I can tell you I think this man is a prophet and nothing good will come of treachery against him."

"Yes, well, as I said, Caiaphas would be greatly pleased if there were proof this man is not a friend of the Jews, and of course we would like to know of anyone breaking the law. Shalom." With that Malchus left to go report to Caiaphas that the tax table and sacrifices were ready as well as the content of his conversation with Father.

It wasn't long before Jesus and his disciples approached the Temple from the road to Bethany. As usual each morning this week, pilgrims along the road recognized him and joined the group and a small crowd of people all came to the Temple as one, singing the psalms of praise heard from pilgrims approaching Jerusalem. After the crowd had entered and I helped sell some sacrificial doves and recorded the transactions in Fathers' ledger to his satisfaction, he let me slip away to my spot between the massive columns to watch and listen to the Rabbi Jesus.

The crowd was gathered around Jesus; some women came and brought their children to be touched by him, others ailing from some affliction asked for healing. This only seemed to annoy a group of Pharisees that always seemed to be gathered on the outskirts of everyone watching. Standing with them today were a few Sadducees and elders, normally all at odds with each other bickering over control of the High Council and Sanhedrin. Today they spoke quietly among themselves and I saw two of them prod a young scribe out to ask a question of Jesus. I recognized the scribe as a Herodian who visited our synagogue one day during my studies. I didn't have a very high opinion of him. After all, a Herodian is a Jew that recognizes Herod Antiphas as tetrarch, or king of Galilee. I couldn't understand how a Jew could be loyal to a king who cut the head off John the Baptist. The Herodian slipped away from the group of Pharisees and approached Jesus from a different side of the crowd.

"Master, we know that thou are true. We know you do not care for the rule of man; for thou regards not the person of men, but teach the way of God in truth. Can you tell us as a Jewish people; is it lawful to give tribute to Caesar? Shall we give or shall we refuse?

Raising his voice just a little more than normal, Jesus replied *"Why do you tempt me? Bring me a penny that I may see it."* And the young Herodian pulled out a coin from his hip pouch. *"Whose image and superscription is this on this penny?"* He asked the crowd gathered around him showing all of them the penny between his fingers. A few from the crowd called out, "It is Caesar." In response Jesus said *"Then render unto Caesar the things that are Caesar's"* paused, turned to place the penny back into the hand of the young Herodian, saying *"and give to God the things that are Gods."* A murmur of satisfaction about his answer was heard gently coursing through the crowd.

Another man approached from the opposite side of the crowd. This one was a Sadducee. All I really knew about the Pharisees and Sadducees was that the Sadducees didn't believe in resurrection after death. I was studying the Torah and practicing my reading and writing, but had never really given much thought to whether there's a resurrection after death. Most of the rabbis I studied with were Pharisees; I would have to remember to bring this topic up next week when I go back to the synagogue. The Sadducee stood and asked "Master, Moses wrote unto us, 'If a man's brother dies, and his wife is left behind without bearing any children, then his brother should take his wife and raise up children unto his brother.' Now suppose there are seven brothers. The first took a wife but died without bearing children. So the second brother took the wife, but he died without leaving children, and the third brother did so likewise. Until the seven brothers all had taken her for a wife without bearing any children. Finally the wife herself died. My question is about the resurrection therefore, when all shall rise, whose wife shall she be of all the brothers? For all seven brothers had married her."

Jesus replied loud enough for the crowd to hear but looked at the Sadducee directly. *"You have erred because you do not know the scriptures nor do you know the power of God."* Now speaking to the crowd, *"The children of this world marry and are given in marriage.*

"But those who will be counted worthy to obtain the other world through the resurrection of the dead, neither marry, nor are women given in marriage. Neither can they die any more; for they are equal unto the angels; they are the children of God, being the children of the resurrection. Have you not read in the book of Moses, how in the bush God spoke unto Moses saying 'I am the God of Abraham, and the God of Isaac, and the God of Jacob?' God is not the God of the dead but the God of the living. The resurrected have life in God. Therefore it is this way you have greatly erred." Jesus was again looking at the Sadducee as he spoke the last part but strolled around everyone, closer to me but still on the edge of the crowd seated around him.

The group of Pharisees and elders in back started talking quietly, a few scribes listened to their discussion and one came forward saying "Master, you have answered us well regarding a most difficult question. Please tell us 'Which is the first commandment of all?'

Jesus answered *"The first of all commandments is, Hear, O Israel; the Lord our God is one Lord: and thou shall love the Lord thy God with all thy heart, with all thy soul, with all thy mind, and with all thy strength. This is the first commandment. The second is very much like the first, namely this; Thou shall love thy neighbor as thyself. There are no other commandments greater than these."*

The scribe replied, "Master, thou has spoken the truth, for there is but one God, and there is none other but He. And to love Him with all thy heart, and understanding, with all thy soul, and with all thy strength, *and* to love his neighbor as himself, well that is worth more than any whole burnt offerings and sacrifices.

"You are not far from the kingdom of God." Jesus said to the scribe now standing directly beside him. The group of Pharisees and elders began distancing themselves from the crowd walking slowly out to the corridor, but before they could leave the courtyard, Jesus turned to them and said *"Tell me, what you think of The Christ? Whose son is he?"* they replied "the son of David, of course."

Turning to the crowd, Jesus asked a question; *"The scribes and Pharisees have studied the Torah, they know scripture. Can anyone tell me how the scribes say that The Christ is the son of David?"* Everyone looked at each other wondering if they should try to answer, but Jesus went on, *"How then does David call him Lord? David himself said; The Lord said to my Lord, Sit thou on my right hand, and I will make thine enemies thy footstool. David himself called him Lord. Therefore, how can The Christ be his son?"*

No one could answer. The Pharisees stood there with an expression of confusion thinking about what was just said. The scribe turned away, his hand rubbing his chin, lost in thought. None of the scribes, Pharisees or Sadducees came forward to ask any more questions. Jesus motioned for his disciples to come closer to the front of the crowd sitting around him and began speaking to everyone.

"The kingdom of heaven is like that of a certain king who had arranged the marriage of his son. But the king was not well liked by his subjects. He sent forth his servants to call on those invited; but they would not come.

Again, he sent forth other servants saying; 'Tell those invited, Behold I have prepared the dinner; my oxen and fatlings have been slaughtered, all things are ready; come unto the marriage.'

But those invited still did not come. They made light of the invitation and went their way, one to his farm; another to their business. And some that remained took his servants and treated them spitefully and slew them.

When the king heard this he became very angry. He sent forth his armies, destroyed the murderers, and burned the city.

But he then said to his servants, 'The wedding is ready, but those that were invited were not worthy. Go therefore into the highways and roads, and bid as many people as you find to come to the wedding ceremony.

So the servants went out into the roads and gathered together as many subjects as they could find, both bad and good people, and the wedding was furnished with guests plenty.

But when the king came in to see the guests, he saw a man had come to the wedding without dressing up in the normal wedding garment. The king asked him 'Friend, why have you come to the feast without dressing yourself in the appropriate wedding garment? But the man was speechless and could not answer.

And the king said to his servants 'Bind him hand and foot, take him away and cast him into the darkness; there shall be weeping and gnashing of teeth. For many are called, but few are chosen.'"

Caiaphas, the elders, scribes and Pharisees standing around, walked away, talking quietly among each other.

I watched Jesus the rest of the morning from my perch between two large marble columns separating the colonnade from the courtyard. He left around lunchtime with his group of disciples heading back up the road toward Bethany. I returned to sit with Father and practice writing, but he immediately put me to work helping sell doves and making notations in the ledger for him.

Late in the afternoon I was strapping the empty dove cages to the mule at the bottom of the stairs. We'd been able to sell all the doves we brought, and Father preferred I start home with the pack mule while he continued working until sundown. During one of my trips up and down the stairs while I was packing the mule, I noticed the disciple named Judas returning from the road to Bethany. He washed his hands, face and feet and passed me going up the stairs as I was carrying the last of our empty dove cages down to the mule. I wondered why he had come back to Temple. I tied the dove cages down and made my way back up the stairs. By the time I returned to the top, I saw Judas walking down the hallway toward Malchus, standing outside the council chamber. My curiosity was getting the best of me. I admired Jesus. I enjoyed listening to his stories, and he also made me think about my Jewish faith, especially since I had been studying for my bar mitzvah. But the elders and priests didn't like him. They questioned his every move and resented him healing the people that came to him. What if he really was the Messiah who would deliver us from the rule of the Roman Empire? The Sanhedrin tried to find a reason to have him arrested after he raised Lazarus, but couldn't even find two men who would speak against him. I slipped past Father and quickly went down the hallway toward the Council Room.

I ducked into the courtyard and was able to find a hiding place between the pillars where I could see the door to the council room. Judas introduced himself to Malchus, "Good evening sir, I believe you're a servant of the High Priest Caiaphas, are you not?" They spoke briefly, and then Malchus entered the council chamber leaving Judas outside. Soon, the door opened and Judas was led inside.

"Good day. My head servant says you have some important news to share?" Caiaphas said.

"I do. I have knowledge of Jesus of Nazareth. I've traveled with him the past few years."

"And who might you be; that you have such knowledge?"

"Judas Iscariot. I've been one of his followers for three years, and have come to be the treasurer among our group. I too, marvel at his deeds. However, I fear his popularity is interfering with his message. I have some concerns."

"Do you believe he is The Christ?" Caiaphas asked.

"It would be foolish for me to say so in your presence." Judas replied knowing the consequences imposed for any Jew saying that. "But *if* he is the Messiah, I think he may need to be prompted into action against our Roman oppressors. Something has to happen."

"So you do believe he is The Christ, the coming Messiah?" Caiaphas prodded.

"I said, *if* he is the Messiah. If so, he should gather the Jewish people together and deliver us from the rule of these pagan Romans. Scripture says the Messiah will be a great warrior of our Jewish people, yet he speaks of turning the other cheek when struck; and of loving your enemy. Just yesterday he allowed a woman to break open an alabaster box of precious spikenard oil and waste it by pouring it over his head. He said she was anointing him. We could have easily sold that oil to provide ourselves food, or help the poor as we often do with whatever money we are given. Yet he allowed her to pour it out over his head. Such a waste! I've begun to have my doubts. I grow tired of just traveling around speaking to crowds of hungry and sick people. "

"Yet you would turn him in to the High Council?" asked Caiaphas.

"It would force him to finally *do* something." Was the reply from Judas. "I'll know where we'll be staying each night. I know the crowds around him present a problem. You can't approach him during the day without making many people angry; so many hang on his every word." Judas replied.

Caiaphas looked at Judas for a moment before responding. "I see how you may question his motives. Can you provide any proof he's conspired against the nation of Israel? Will you testify that he's called himself king of the Jews? Can you provide testimony that he's blasphemed?" Caiaphas seemed to be pushing for something more serious against Jesus other than wasting expensive spikenard oil.

"No, no. I can't testify against him. I won't. I can only say I know how to lead you to him. I know where he's been staying this week, and will know where he will be in the coming days. I'm sure we can come to an agreement over the value of such information."

"Yes, I'm sure we can. So I'll tell you what the Sanhedrin would prefer. We don't want to upset the people. We must be able to take him alone, after dark, away from crowds. And not before the Passover feast. It'd be best to take him when many pilgrims have departed Jerusalem, but certainly before he leaves Jerusalem himself. Do you think you can provide this service to the Sanhedrin?"

"Quite easily." Judas replied.

"And the price for your services? Shall we say twenty pieces of silver?"

"It's worth twice that. After all, you have sought ways to arrest him for almost a year without success. I'm offering to lead your men straight to him."

"Thirty pieces of silver. That's my final offer." Caiaphas retorted. "It'll happen with or without your help. You're providing nothing but expedience. Tell me now before I get bored."

"That's sufficient. How shall I seek you out when the time has come?"

"Seek out my head servant." Turning to Malchus Caiaphas said, "Show him where your quarters are and make yourself available should he knock after dark. If he shows up to lead us to Jesus, go with him and take a band of guards with you. We'll find people willing to testify to words of blasphemy later. First we arrest him."

The council room door opened and Judas emerged, Malchus following close behind. I was still hiding behind the column.

"When do you think the time will be right?" Malchus asked as the two stood outside the council chamber door.

"Late Wednesday, after Seder supper. He has a fondness for spending time in the garden of Gethsemane. I'm inclined to believe we'll be camped there before leaving Jerusalem. Even if we're offered housing somewhere, I'll be able to lead you directly to him before we leave Jerusalem. Tell your guards the man I kiss hello in greeting will be Jesus of Nazareth."

"A kiss. Yes. An appropriate sign for the guards to take action. Come, let me show you where to contact me at night."

Malchus said and started to walk down the corridor. Judas turned and followed.

I sat still, quiet, holding my breath. Thoughts raced through my mind. Should I tell Father what I overheard? Maybe I could find Jesus and warn him that one of his own had just agreed to turn him over to the Sanhedrin. I could approach Jesus while he's teaching here tomorrow. What would I say? Would he believe a child? Why would one of his own followers want him arrested? What law had he broken? I was lost in my thoughts as I rose and started quickly walking to the entry where Father sat collecting the Temple tax. I'll speak with him tonight after dinner. Surely Father wouldn't think Jesus deserved to be arrested. I wondered if he could do anything about it? I stopped by the table but Father was busy and couldn't talk so I just said Shalom and started down the stairs. The mule was still tied up with empty dove cages strapped across its back. I untied him and tugged on the reins to head up the road to Bethany. I was unaware of anything around me as the questions in my mind sought unfound answers. I had not seen that I was being watched.

Malchus had noticed a shadow across the hallway floor, like a bump on the column as the daylight shone between the two columns, a shadow that shouldn't be there, small and odd. Malchus turned to walk down the corridor expecting Judas to follow. After a step he looked over his shoulder toward the odd shaped shadow, watching for its creator. He stopped for a second, allowed Judas to pass him, and recognized the boy Jonas, son of the Temple tax collector Abram, scurrying through the Temple courtyard toward the entry not far from where he stood.

Malchus caught up with Judas, and continued down the

hall finally approaching the table of Abram. He watched Jonas pass by, yell Shalom and trot down the stairs. They stood at the top of the stairs.

"My quarters are located in that small building across the avenue." Malchus said, pointing to a long one-storied building across the street. Jonas was now trotting down the last flight of steps toward the mule loaded with empty dove cages. "See the bush on the corner? That corner apartment is mine." Malchus said pointing so Judas would know where to find him when the time came, never taking his eyes off Jonas, tugging on the mule, pulling it toward the road to Bethany. Had the boy heard anything? What of it if he did, Malchus wondered. He had to have heard something. Why was the boy hurrying? Why had he been hiding? Eavesdropping. He must have heard been eavesdropping, he heard something.

"Shalom, Malchus. Perhaps I will seek you out late Wednesday after Seder supper, perhaps early Thursday before sunrise. Have the silver and authorities ready for my return and Caiaphas will be pleased." Judas said as he turned to walk down the stairs

"Shalom" Malchus answered, lost in his own thoughts of Jonas and wondering what to do about this young boy who had apparently overheard the plans to have Jesus arrested. 'Have the silver and authorities ready and Caiaphas will be pleased.' The words echoed through his head. Malchus had worked his way up to head servant by making sure his master was always well pleased. A few luxuries came with being head servant, not to mention the occasional payoff from merchants for preferential treatment, or referrals he made that proved profitable. Caiaphas was serious this time. He'd wanted Jesus arrested since last years Passover feast. Caiaphas asked the Romans to question citizens about Jesus breaking laws, and no one could testify against him. The Romans laughed at Caiaphas. They had the nerve to ask if Caiaphas agreed Jesus was the so-called Christ. Caiaphas was livid for a week after that. No, Caiaphas wanted Jesus arrested this year, and I, Malchus, will do everything necessary to make sure it happens. Jonas continued to tug on the mule headed up the road to Bethany. Malchus thought to himself 'I know that road. It grows into a hilly, rocky road. There are places where an accident might easily happen. The mule is slowing him down too. I could easily pass him without being seen. Perhaps I could simply question him to find out what he heard. No, I'm sure he heard us. Now we have a plan, and I have to make it happen. We have the means at our disposal. Caiaphas will be pleased when he finds out what I'm capable and willing to do. There's really only one thing I must do. I must stop the boy Jonas from reaching his home.

I tugged on the mule heading home, thinking about all I'd heard and wondering why Caiaphas, the Priests, the Pharisees and all the elders seemed to hate Jesus so much. They were going to have him arrested. He has done nothing wrong. What could I do? I wished I could have waited on Father to return home. I needed to tell someone. I knew I could tell Mother as soon as I got home. She would help. The mule was starting to settle in to a slow steady gait without my constant pulling on the reins and I was heading into the hills outside Jerusalem, on the road to Bethpage.

I headed up a second hill about a third of the way home. The terrain was rockier now and the road often hugged the hill, falling steeply off one side. The mule and I continued our journey home; all the while I was trying to understand why the leaders of our people wanted Jesus arrested. Perhaps I was lost in my own thoughts, distracting me from being aware of things around me. Maybe I heard some kind of noise as I passed by a large rock outcrop from the hill to my right, but I was too busy thinking through all my questions, thinking about unpacking the mule quickly, feeding him, and asking mother how to get Father involved to prevent the arrest of Jesus. Then everything went black as Malchus, the head servant of the High Priest Caiaphas, slammed a rock into the back of my head. As I lay on the ground, he grabbed my head, twisted sharply, and hard; and the sound of bone breaking echoed through my skull. He dragged me across the road and threw me down the steep hill on the left side of the road, into a ravine. Malchus looked down at my lifeless body, and turned to go back to the Temple.

Tuesday

Father found the mule standing by themselves on the road home right before sundown last night. He was frantic looking for me, shouting my name, running up and down the road. I could "see" him, as if I were floating above him, watching it all happen. I'd never seen Father scared of anything, but he looked afraid now. And the anguished cry I "heard" from him as he saw my mangled body laying a short way down the hill was something strange and foreign to me. He brought my limp body up, tearing the empty dove cages off the mule and placing me across its back. Everything in my house stopped as we returned home. Relatives gathered around to comfort Mother.

My older cousin was sent out to tell other family members of the tragedy. My aunt took mother, wailing and screaming, away from my lifeless body and returned by herself to prepare my body for burial.

I was buried Tuesday afternoon, after my body had been cleaned and rubbed with oil and the tomb prepared. I was wrapped in new white burial linens that had been purchased for my grandfather. The men gathered around our family tomb. My two uncles and older cousin sat there outside singing psalms to God celebrating my life and my return to our maker no matter how short my stay here had been. My Father of course was there though I could see he wasn't singing very much. He often broke down crying stepping away from the others to hide his tears. The women of Bethpage came in procession to the tomb after I had been buried, and a stone put in front of the entrance. They wailed all along the path to the sepulcher. My sister was among them though not yet a woman. She and I had not yet turned thirteen. She cried constantly. I wanted to hug her and tell her I felt no pain. I was anxiously waiting to meet God. I wanted to comfort those who mourned so for me.

Wednesday

"The scribes and Pharisees sit in Moses' seat. Therefore, whatever they bid of you, you should do and observe. But be careful, do not follow in their ways, do not do what they do, for they say well and teach well, but their behavior does not reflect what they teach.

They bind people with heavy burdens, rules, duties and responsibilities to be borne. They lay these burdens on men's shoulders, but they themselves will not lift one finger to move them. They perform their works so they may be seen by others; they make broad their phylacteries and enlarge the borders of their garments to show their status. They love the uppermost room at the feasts; the best seats at the synagogue; the recognition and greetings from the people in their daily life. They love to be called Rabbi.

But do not wish to be called Rabbi, for only one is your master, that is The Christ, and all of you are brothers. In the same manner, call no man your Father here on earth, for only one is your Father and He is in heaven.

Nor Masters, be not called Master, for you have only one master; that is The Christ.
And he that is greatest among you shall be your servant.
And whosoever shall exalt himself shall be abased. He that humbles himself shall be exalted.
Woe unto you scribes and Pharisees, you hypocrites! You devour the houses of widows; you take their property to pay debts of their husbands and in pretense say long prayers for them. For this you shall receive greater damnation. You shut up

the kingdom of heaven against all men; you neither go into the kingdom of heaven yourself and you rail against men trying to enter.

Woe unto you, scribes and Pharisees as you compass the sea and land to make one proselyte, and when he is made, you make him twice the child of hell than you are yourselves.

Woe unto you blind guides of the people. You tell them 'Whosoever shall swear by the Temple is nothing, but whosoever swears by the gold of the Temple, well he is the one to receive rewards.' Which is greater, the gold, or the Temple which sanctifies the gold? They say whosoever swears by the altar, it is nothing, but should that person swear by the gift placed on the altar, well he is worthy. You fools and blind leaders; which is greater; the gift, or the altar that sanctifies the gift? Whoever swears by the altar, swears by it and all things on it, And whoever swears by the Temple swears by it and by Him that dwells within it."

Jesus had been strolling around the edge of the crowd seated before him. Often he would look directly at one of the small cliques of elders, Pharisees, scribes, or Sadducees. They stood together in their own little groups, whispering to each other on occasion, especially whenever Jesus called out 'hypocrite!' He was now standing near an entry into the great courtyard. Directly across the colonnade from the doorway was the treasury donation table, and Jesus watched a few minutes as people donated money to the treasury of the Temple. More than once in just a few minutes, a man of wealth would make a donation to the Temple treasury, and somehow you could tell they wanted you to know it was a great amount they were donating. Some slowly dropped their half shekels into the treasury box, as if someone watching might try to count the number donated. Others made a small scene so you would notice they were donating whole shekels rather than the common half shekel. And then a small woman walked up to the box, bent over in her old age, pulled out two mites, a mere farthing, from a ragged leather pouch, donated them and walked away.

Jesus pulled one of his disciples from his seat in the crowd; the one called Judas. He pointed over to the old woman and said to everyone listening,

"Verily I say unto you. This poor widow has cast more into the treasury than the wealthy men; more than all the wealthy have donated. For all that they cast in to offerings of God came from their abundance. The widow lives in poverty and she gave from all that she had to live on.

Woe unto you scribes and Pharisees for being hypocrites. You pay tithes of mint, anise and cumin, but omit the weightier matters of the law, judgment, mercy and faith. That is what's important. You are blind guides that strain at a gnat but swallow a camel.

Woe unto you scribes and Pharisees who make a show of cleaning the outside of the cup and platter, while within it is full of extortion and excess. Cleanse first the inside of the cup, that the outside may also become clean.

Woe unto you blind scribes and Pharisees, hypocrites! You are like the white sepulchers, the grand looking coffins, appearing beautiful outward but within are full of dead men's bones and of all uncleanness. Outwardly you appear righteous unto men, but within you are full of hypocrisy and iniquity.

Woe unto you, scribes and Pharisees you hypocrites, because you build the tombs of the prophets and decorate the

coffins of the righteous. Then you say 'If we had only been alive in the days of our Fathers, we would not have been partakers with them in the blood of these prophets. But look at yourselves, you are the children of those which killed the prophets, and you have been filled with the same attitudes and behaviors of your Fathers. How then can you escape the damnation of hell?*

Wherefore, behold, I send unto you prophets, and wise men, and scribes; and some of them you shall kill and crucify, and some of them you will scourge in your synagogues; you will persecute them from city to city.

That upon you may come all the righteous blood shed upon the earth; from the blood of righteous Abel unto the blood of Zacharias; son of Barachias, whom you slew between the Temple and the altar. Verily I say unto you, all these things shall come upon this generation.

O Jerusalem, Jerusalem! Thou that kills the prophets, and stones those sent to thee. How often I have gathered thy children together; even as a hen gathers her chicks under her wing?

But you do not! Your house is left unto you desolate.

For I say unto you, you shall not see me henceforth, until you shall say, 'Blessed is he that cometh in the name of the Lord.'"

Jesus turned and walked out the entry into the grand corridor, his disciples scrambling to rise and follow.

Without knowing it, Sarah was watching Jesus from between the same marble pillars I sat between when I watched and listened this past week. She had made her way from the family shortly after noon, quietly, without anyone noticing, after feeding the animals. Everyone was quiet, quietly sobbing or loudly wailing along with mother over the tragic accident that took the life of her young son. No one noticed Sarah was missing. My aunts took control of preparing the meal since mother was so grief-stricken. Sarah told my older cousin where she was going in case someone should notice her missing, but she didn't tell him her plans. Now she sat between the same columns I had sat, listening to Jesus, trying to muster up the courage to speak to him, not knowing what she was going to say. As Jesus spoke his final words and turned to walk away, she herself turned and ran toward the northern Gate of Israel, the gate for women. She realized she had to hurry down those stairs and around the corner of the Temple where Jesus would be exiting from the Gate of Gentiles. She had to catch up to him and speak with him.

She caught sight of Jesus and his group of followers as she rounded the corner of the Temple. Only his disciples had followed him out of the Temple though he had been speaking to a large group gathered around him in the courtyard. They started up the road to Bethany and Sarah followed a short distance behind. The group had climbed the first hill of the road, stopped and turned around. Jesus was speaking to his disciples now, and he seemed to be talking about the Temple. She saw him spread out his arms as if he were caressing the beautiful vision before him. Once she thought she was seen. But instead she saw two of his disciples depart the group and head back toward her and Jerusalem. Sarah quickened her pace as she started up the hill, knowing that the family sepulcher was not so far away and Jesus was even closer. She had to speak with him.

Jesus and his disciples were gathered at the top of the hill, resting, looking out at the city of Jerusalem and the gold dome of the Temple in the distance. She didn't know they were waiting for the two disciples to return to take them to a house where they would be celebrating the Passover Seder Supper. Timidly, but with steely resolve, Sarah approached the group until, reaching them, she fell to her knees before Jesus. She thought hard and remembered what the blind man Bartimaeus said. She swallowed, and spoke in a clear voice "Son of David, have mercy on me."

One of the disciples spoke sharply at her lying prostrate on the ground, saying "Child, what is the meaning of this? Get up, go home, you shouldn't be out here unescorted. Leave! Do not bother him. Go home now!" But all Sarah could think to do was say "Son of David, have mercy on me!" in the strongest voice she could muster. Her assertiveness surprised herself, she would not normally dare speak first to a man, much less a stranger. Nor would she ever disobey an adult. But she refused to move and gathered the courage to speak again. "Son of David, have mercy on me."

Jesus said to her *"What is it my child?"*

Her words now came forth with confidence and heartbreaking sorrow. "Master, Son of David, please hear my plea. My twin brother has died just two days ago. He had been listening to you every day this week. He's told me the stories you have spoken to the people here in the Temple. He said you have healed people, many people. I believe anything is possible through you, I've seen the miracle of Lazarus from the village of Bethany. I know you can do the same for my brother if only you would say the word. Son of David, have mercy on me, please. Please help my brother."

Another disciple started to object "Child, get up..." but Jesus cut him off mid-sentence, *"Stop! There is time for this child. Our room for the Passover meal is not yet prepared, and we are still waiting the return of Thomas. Stay here and I'll return shortly."* With that, Jesus offered Sarah his hand to help her up saying, *"Child, show me the tomb."*

Sarah stood, saying "Thank you, son of David, thank you. This way, the family tomb is not far down this road." She started up the road toward Bethany with Jesus following close behind. After a short distance, they came upon the spot where Malchus had ambushed Jonas two days earlier. She slowed down, turned to Jesus with tears in her eyes, "This is where Father found Jonas; in that ravine." pointing down the steep hill off the side of the road. "His neck was broken in the fall, but we don't know how he fell." She turned and continued up the road. Not much further, she turned right, off the road, onto a path leading up a hill, dense with trees on either side. Large rocks and boulders could be seen among the trees as they climbed to reach a clearing in front of a small cave. Sarah's family used this cave as their tomb. The path Sarah took ended here at the clearing. Another path intersected; one direction leading up a hill to their family olive grove on the other side which was the hill facing their house. The other direction led down to the Cedron Valley, and the Garden of Gethsemane on the opposite hillside.

As Sarah and Jesus approached the cave, a great cry was heard as if coming from the tomb itself. Sarah wondered if it could be Jonas though she knew better. She thought it sounded like Jonas, she thought she heard the word 'Hosanna' but wasn't sure. Jesus took hold of the rock in front of the small cave entrance and pulled on it to roll it away from the opening. Crouching down to his knees, he crawled into the cave to retrieve the body of Jonas wrapped in fine burial lines. Pulling the body out into the clearing, loosening the wrap and removing the fine linen face covering, Jesus spread out his arms, lifted them up to the sky, and said in a clear voice *"Father in heaven, in your name all things are possible."* He then reached down, took Jonas by the hand, commanded, *"Rise! Jonas, your work here has not yet begun."*

With that, Jonas opened his eyes and gasped in a large breath of air. Jesus helped him sit upright. Jonas covered his eyes from the light of day with one hand while leaning back supported by his other arm. Sarah had been kneeling beside them on the ground weeping until she saw her brother take in his breath of newborn life. She covered her mouth in awe then excitedly blurted out "Jonas, you're alive! You're alive! Jesus has raised you from the grave! Jonas you're alive!" She leaped to hug him knocking him backward to the ground as she did so.

I'm Alive

It seemed as if I had been woken from a deep sleep. I heard my name called and as if in a dream, I turned toward the sound. I was immediately blinded by the suddenness of light and overwhelmed by the sensation of air rushing into my lungs filling the emptiness swiftly. My mind was groggy and my first thoughts were to wonder where I was. I could feel the hand of someone helping me sit up and feel the wrap of a linen sheet around my body. Where were my clothes? I heard Sarah's excited words that I was alive; Jesus had raised me from the grave, and a vague memory of the blow to my head swept through my mind. Then I was knocked backward as Sarah wrapped her arms around me in a hug so tight I thought she would squeeze the air back out of my lungs. I sensed it was late in the afternoon. While embraced in the arms of Sarah I looked up to see the face of Jesus smiling down at me. *"Rest here Jonas, and gather your strength. You have a long life yet to live; your time has not yet come. From this day forward, you shall be called Mark, and one day your words will guide the world. Return to your family. Live, learn and love, for your work here has just begun."*

Jesus knelt beside us as he said this. He stood to leave and I started to panic. I felt such a fear growing inside me I blurted out "Wait! Don't leave me. I want to go with you. I can't go home. And they're going to arrest you! I heard them! Caiaphas means to harm you!" I didn't know if I was afraid for Jesus or for myself and my newfound life. I recognized I was sitting on the ground outside our family tomb, and the understanding that I had died and been raised from the dead just like Lazarus filled me with fear and confusion. But I had been able to warn Jesus about his pending arrest. Maybe everything would be okay now. Maybe he could avoid trouble with Caiaphas and the Sanhedrin. Maybe he wouldn't be arrested.

Jesus turned to me, smiled and said, *"As your work here has not yet begun, my work here is not finished. I must go now. You will know what to do. Do not be afraid. Peace be with you, Mark."* He turned and started back down the trail. Sarah was kneeling beside me now and asked "What does he mean by your work has not begun?"

"I don't know Sarah. And he called me Mark. All his disciples said they had another name before following Jesus. Maybe I'll become a follower as well."

"No Jonas! You must come home. Now! Father and mother will be so happy. They're so sad and heart-broken. You must come home now, while we still have daylight, come!"

"But I have no clothes; it still hurts when I try to move. Sarah; go get Father. I'll stay here and wait. I need to gather my strength. Bring me back some clothes and sandals. Please. It won't take long."

"No, Jonas."

"Call me Mark."

"No, Jonas. Come home now! You must try."

"I said call me Mark. My name is Mark now. He said my name was Mark!" I started to rise and fell back to the ground sitting up. "See, I can't go anywhere yet. I'm too weak to move. Go get help and I'll be here when you get back. Sarah, please. Let me rest and gather my strength."

"No. You'll just leave to go find Jesus. You must come home. Now!" raising her voice suspecting what I really had in mind.

"I can't, Sarah. It hurts when I move. Go before you lose daylight."

After some more pleading, I finally convinced Sarah to go home to get help. But she knew me too well; she is my twin after all. I *was* going to find Jesus somehow. After she left, I wrapped the burial linen around me, trying to make it fit as a toga would though I had no sash to tie around my waist. It did hurt when I moved so I sat there for a little while thinking about how I was going to find Jesus. Sarah told me I had been dead for two days but I hadn't put it together that today was Passover and Holy week would be ending. I thought Jesus would be back at the Temple tomorrow teaching the people. I knew I didn't want to go home tonight. If that happened, they wouldn't let me leave tomorrow to find Jesus. So there was only one thing I thought I could do. I had to hide out tonight somewhere I wouldn't be found. I would go into Jerusalem tomorrow and beg Jesus to take me in as a follower and disciple. I had to try at least. He is The Christ and I have no choice but to follow Him. I'll worry about convincing my parents later. First I had to convince Jesus and his disciples.

The sun was slowly moving lower in the sky and I knew Sarah would be coming back with Father. I started feeling a sense of urgency to move. For a second I thought I could wait on clothes and sandals, and convince Father that I needed to find Jesus. But as soon as I had that thought I knew he wouldn't hear of it. Nor would Mother allow me to leave the family again. Mother wouldn't allow me to leave tomorrow even if it was to find Jesus. I had to leave now. If it meant camping out in the Garden of Gethsemane tonight, so be it. I would find Jesus tomorrow at the Temple, just as he is every day. I gathered my strength and started down the trail into the valley. I knew I could rest in the Garden of Gethsemane tonight if I could make it that far.

Moving was difficult. My muscles ached with a stiffness that made it easier to move taking small slow deliberate steps. The linen I wore didn't impede me, though I wished I had a heavier toga for warmth, and sandals too. Slowly I climbed down the hill and continued on a path toward the Garden of Gethsemane. The Garden was about half way up the other side of the hill if my memory was correct. There was a path from there leading to another road to Jerusalem. But I knew I would be able to camp out safely in the Garden. No one would think of looking for me there. I felt badly that my parents would soon be very angry with me. But I had to speak with Jesus before returning home. I'll go back home, but first I had to find Jesus. I had to speak with Him.

The walk across the valley and up the hill to Gethsemane seemed to take hours before I saw the bushes and flora of the garden. The sun had set and I would stop every now and then to catch my breath. I know Father would have been angry when Sarah brought him back to an empty tomb. At least he would know I wasn't dead. Maybe Mother could also take comfort in that thought and not be so angry with me. I continued moving slowly up the path, in darkness toward the Garden of Gethsemane.

In The Garden

From my hiding spot here I see Malchus, fallen and kneeling on the ground clutching his right ear, blood staining his fingers and hands. He's kneeling there wild-eyed. His sobbing has stopped and he is frantically feeling the side of his head. He's just staring at Jesus being led away by the guards, eyes wide, mouth open. I don't understand this confused look on his face. Then I see the side of his head and his ear, fully intact, not dangling by the sliver of skin like it was seconds ago. His ear is fully healed now, the bleeding has stopped. He kneels there no longer wild-eyed from the shock of having his ear cut off, but from the shock of having it healed. He was healed instantly when Jesus touched his ear, the man he worked so hard to get arrested had healed him.

Or maybe he's looking a little wild-eyed because he's happened to see me crouching beside this bush watching the whole scene. What? How? The very boy he chased; the very boy he caught; the very boy he killed. He snapped my neck like a chicken and threw me down that hill. How could this be? He had walked up to my unconscious body lying on the roadside after hitting me with a rock, grabbed my head and twisted my neck until he heard that final snap. He made everything look like an accident, and made sure I told no one about the plan to arrest Jesus. He's seen me now and he is again wild-eyed with his own fear. He points up with his right hand, his eyes filled with confusion and disbelief, knowing I died a few days ago, knowing he killed me, knowing I knew the truth and must be stopped, miracle or no miracle. He pointed up at me for the two Roman guards to grab.

Two guards lunged at me. I stumbled backward from the bush I was hiding behind. I tried to run away, my legs twisting and turning awkwardly without the coordination I was so used to knowing just last week. I felt the sharpness of the roots on the soles of my feet, yet felt no pain as I ran, tried to run, tried to escape their grasp. Grabbing my arms, they seized me by the burial linen that was to be my garment for eternity. It was made from fine cloth, exquisitely woven for the burial of a beloved family member. The garment was now partly on the ground under foot and partly twisted around the legs of the guards grabbing me. I turned and contorted in my struggle to free my body from their grasp. The very linen that was to comfort me through my timeless journey now wrapped its weave around the legs of the guards. The threads loosened their grip on me, growing tighter around the legs of the guards; as if moving on its own volition, letting me free, enabling my escape from its clutches and the arms of the guards. I ran only one step before stumbling to my knees. I lurched forward and sprang upward, my legs trying to move as fast as they could. Looking back; I see the fine linen wrapped around the legs of the two Roman guards. They're rolling on the ground trying to break free from the wrap that has fallen them like an ax to a tree. I was free. I was naked, but at least I was free. And I was alive. Again.
But now my name is Mark.

ABOUT THE AUTHOR

I was born November 28, 1956 in Fountainebleu, France to Army Sergeant Harold Joseph and Anna Mae Perry. Growing up in a practicing Roman Catholic family of two girls and two boys. I graduated from the Georgia Institute of Technology with a B.S. in Industrial Management in 1978.

I have always had a healthy dose of Faith. Jesus has always been my hero. And I have been changed by the power and grace of reconciliation and confession through the Catholic church.

This story came to me as a result of my fascination with verses 51 and 52 of chapter 14 of the Gospel of Mark. The lines about the boy wrapped in linens. This boy was not mentioned in any other Gospel and I wondered for years about him. To satisfy my own curiosity, I thought about the possibilities of his "story" and wrote this as a result of researching the New Testament, politics, and society during the time Jesus walked and taught in the Temple. I truly hope you have enjoyed this piece of fiction and hopefully it has deepened an understanding of the politics and events of Holy Week, the week prior to the crucifixion.

Email me at dperry801@gmail.com for any correspondence and inquiries. And most of all, thank you for your purchase and support.

Dan Perry

Made in the USA
Lexington, KY
09 April 2016